#1

JUNIOR HIGH

JUNIOR
HIGH
JITTERS

D0775741

JUNIOR HIGH

#1

JUNIOR HIGH

JUNIOR HIGH JITTERS

Kate Kenyon

SCHOLASTIC INC.
New York Toronto London Auckland Sydney

ISBN 0-590-41497-6

12 11 10 9 8 7 6 5 4 3 2 1   7 8 9/8 0 1/9

Printed in the U.S.A.   01

First Scholastic printing, October 1986

Chapter 1

"There's something in my Jell-O," Jennifer Mann said. She peered suspiciously at a squiggly orange blob on her plate and tried not to gag.

"You're crazy, Jen," Nora Ryan said good-naturedly. "Even the cafeteria people can't ruin Jell-O. Meat loaf, yes. Jell-O, no."

Nora smiled what she thought was a kindly smile at a group of seventh-graders who were squeezed into a narrow table next to the serving line. They looked cramped and uncomfortable, and Nora remembered that she and Jennifer used to sit in that exact same spot.

That's all behind us, Nora thought happily. This year we can sit wherever we want! It was an unwritten law at Cedar Groves Junior High that the best tables —

the oversized ones in the center of the cafeteria — were reserved for eighth-graders.

Nora pushed a lock of curly brown hair
out of her brown eyes and accidentally
jostled Jennifer's tray. Jen had been her
very best friend for years, but sometimes
she could strangle her. Take today, for
example. How could Jen worry about a
little thing like Jell-O when it was their
very first day back at school! Nora felt too
keyed up to eat — all she wanted to do was
get to one of those center tables and see all
their friends. I won't really feel like an
eighth-grader until I sit down, she decided.

"Jen," Nora said patiently, "you're holding up the line. And all because of a dish
of Jell-O."

"I tell you, there's something in there,"
Jennifer said stubbornly. She handed Nora
a fork. "You can see for yourself."

"If you insist." At times like this, it was
best to humor Jen. Nora made a tentative
stab at the Jell-O when suddenly a mop of
red hair and freckles appeared beside her.
She shuddered inwardly. Jason Anthony.

"What's the trouble, girls?" Jason had
jumped the line, as usual, and was sliding
his tray along the stainless steel dividing
rail. "Ah," he said. "I think I've spotted
the problem." He held the Jell-O up to the
light. "Jennifer Mann, this is your lucky

day. You've got a winged raisin in your dessert!"

"A winged raisin?" Jen asked, puzzled.

"I think he means a fly," Nora said weakly. "Just forget it and keep moving, Jen," she pleaded. At the rate they were going, all their friends would be finished eating by the time they sat down.

"No problem. We can fix this in a minute," Jason promised, a wide grin spreading over his face. "A little sleight of hand, and your Jell-O is turned into . . . a banana pudding!" In one swift movement, he deposited the Jell-O back on the counter, and plunked a heavy dish on Jennifer's tray.

"But I don't even *like* banana pudding," Jennifer protested.

"Really?" Jason's smile grew even wider, and Nora braced herself. Jason was about to do something indescribably gross. She just knew it.

"You should give it a try. It's delicious." Before either of the girls could stop him, Jason stuck his finger in the pudding and licked it, grinning like a hyena.

"Disgusting," Jennifer muttered.

"That kid is defective," Nora said with a sigh. "It's too bad he can't be recalled, like a car." She looked longingly at the center table and nudged Jennifer's tray along. "Can we *please* hurry up?" she pleaded. "All the good seats will be taken!"

"I've never known anyone as impatient as you," Jennifer said to her friend. "We're going to be in school with these kids for a whole year — what's the rush?"

"But it won't be the same as today," Nora objected. "This is our first day as eighth-graders — probably the most exciting day of our whole lives," she said.

Jennifer looked at Nora with disbelief and reached for her change purse. If Nora ever changed her mind about being a doctor, she could have a great career on the stage, she decided.

Jennifer grinned and paid the cashier. "Then don't let *me* be the one to spoil your big day," she said decisively. "Let's go!"

Nora was shorter than Jen, so it was easy for Jen to push her to the center table.

"I can't believe you spent your summer on a farm," Jennifer said to Lucy Armanson a few minutes later. She and Nora had grabbed the last two seats at the table and were shouting to be heard over the noise of banging trays and silverware. Lucy shook her curly black Afro and grinned. "You mean I don't look like a country girl?" she challenged.

Jennifer's hazel eyes swept over Lucy's tailored linen pants and hand-knit sweater.

Lucy, with her slim figure and high cheek-bones, looked like she had just stepped off the pages of a fashion magazine. "Nope. You're just not the type for bib overalls," she said, digging into her salad.

"Not unless they're from Paris," Tracy Douglas added.

"You should know," Susan Hillard said sarcastically. "You never wear anything unless it's got an alligator or a swan plastered across it." Susan gave a smug smile and nibbled her tuna sandwich as Tracy flushed.

"Why are you always so mean to me?" Tracy protested. "I don't go out of my way to buy them, it's just that — " She broke off suddenly and stared over Nora's shoulder. "Who's the blonde girl at the next table?" she asked in a loud whisper. "I haven't seen her before."

"Which one?" Jennifer said automatically, as four heads swung around. Then she caught sight of shimmering golden hair touching lightly tanned shoulders. Her first thought was: How could anyone look that good from the back? The girl turned just then and Jennifer was awed by a pair of clear blue eyes, a perfect nose, and full lips accented in pale pink gloss. She was the most beautiful girl Jennifer had ever seen, and she nearly gasped in surprise. "Oh, wow," she added, "that one!"

"Yeah, that one," Lucy said wryly. She lowered her voice and leaned across the table. *"That* is her highness, Denise Hendrix."

"Her highness?" Tracy said in a hushed tone. "You mean she's really a princess or something?" Tracy believed everything anyone said.

"Don't be silly,".Susan Hillard snapped. "She's not a princess. It's just Lucy's idea of a joke, and not a very good one." Susan stared coldly across the table. "I know all about her. She's a transfer student from Switzerland." She paused for a moment, and took a sip of milk. "Her father sells . . . cosmetics."

"Sells cosmetics!" Lucy hooted with laughter. "You make him sound like the Avon lady. Listen, I got all the information from the office." She nodded her head toward Denise. "Her family owns Denise Cosmetics. It's one of the biggest companies in the world, and they are *rich!*"

Tracy whispered, "If she's so rich, why does she look so bored?"

Lucy sneaked a quick look at Denise's perfect profile, and then turned back to Tracy. "Think about it," she said seriously. "If you'd been living it up in Europe and you suddenly ended up at Cedar

Groves Junior High, wouldn't you be bored?"

"I'd be bored to pieces," Tracy said solemnly.

Lucy leaned forward and reached for an apple. "I rest my case."

It's the noise, Denise said silently. That's what's really driving me crazy. This has got to be the noisiest school in the world. First the locker doors banging all morning, and now the metal trays slamming against the Formica tables. . . .

She sighed and unconsciously rubbed the slim gold bracelet her father had brought back from a business trip to Paris. Denise Cosmetics had branches around the world, and the family had moved over a dozen times. Denise had lived all over Europe — in London hotels, in French chateaux, and German palaces, but she had never seen anything like Cedar Groves Junior High, she decided.

It was more than the noise, of course. It was the food, the people, the atmosphere. The atmosphere! She smiled when she thought of what Madame Lamarte would say about the steamy cafeteria, with its water-stained ceiling. Madame Lamarte, the proper headmistress of the Swiss boarding school where Denise had spent the last two years, was a perfectionist. According to Madame, dining should be "an experience," and meals at the school were always served with elegant china and crystal. In fact, she had once said that paper napkins marked the decline of a civilization.

"How's it going?" a deep male voice asked. Denise looked up to see her brother Tony peering down at her. He was a sophomore at Cedar Groves High School, which was right next door.

"How do you *think* it's going?" she said sadly. "Are you going to have lunch now?" she asked hopefully. She wasn't thrilled to be seen sitting with her sixteen-year-old brother, but anything would be better than eating in this awful place alone.

" 'Fraid not," Tony said casually. "I just dropped by to see how you were doing." She noticed that he was holding a sandwich and a can of Coke. "I've got a meeting with the counselor at twelve-thirty, so I've got to eat this on the run." He reached over and rumpled her hair, the way he used to when they were little kids. "Hey, cheer up, it's not the end of the world, you know."

"No?" she asked sadly.

"No." He laughed. "Okay, I admit Cedar Groves isn't what we're used to, but we'll get into the swing of it."

"Maybe you will," Denise retorted, "but give me Lucerne anytime."

"You know Dad wanted us to grow up as Americans," Tony said, his face suddenly serious. "He never would have dragged us back here, if it wasn't really important to him. Just keep an open mind, okay?" When she didn't answer, he sighed and popped the tab on his Coke. "Who knows, you might even get to like it here."

"Don't hold your breath," Denise said crisply.

The bell rang then, and Tony moved aside as three girls made their way down the aisle. Denise heard one of them whisper "hunk" as she looked right at Tony. Hunk? she thought, puzzled. What a funny expression. Was Tony a "hunk"? The terrible thing was that there wasn't even anyone here she could ask. She felt lonelier than ever.

"She's with a really cute boy," Tracy said in hushed tones. "Don't turn around, Nora, but he's about six feet tall with black hair and dark eyes, and he's wearing a white sweater. And — uh-oh, too bad, he's leaving. Oh well, easy come, easy go." She giggled.

"I wasn't going to turn around," Nora said, without looking up from her spaghetti and meatballs. "I don't know why you're all making such a fuss over that girl anyway. Or him." Tracy, a pretty blonde girl, was a puzzle to Nora. She was the only one of their group who was undeniably boy-crazy, and as Susan Hillard once said, "would flirt with anything that moved."

"Because he's great-looking," Tracy said with a grin. "And she's really beautiful and mysterious . . . and because all the boys at the next table are staring at her," she added wistfully. "Some girls have all the luck."

"She doesn't look too thrilled to be here," Jennifer whispered. She sneaked another peek at Denise, who was staring off into space. Jason Anthony, terminal creep, and Mitch Pauley, superjock, were blowing straw wrappers in her direction, but she ignored them and they fell harmlessly on the floor.

"Well, I'm sure glad to be here," Nora said, twirling her spaghetti on her fork and smiling happily. "I feel like I've waited all my life to be in eighth grade, and I plan on enjoying every minute of it."

"I can't believe you're eating spaghetti," Susan Hillard's whiny voice cut across the table. "I thought you were on a perpetual health kick."

Nora, refusing to let even Susan annoy

her, said, "It's unbleached spaghetti." She added in a superior tone, "So all the nutrients are still there. It's really a fantastic source of complex carbohydrates."

"Do we have to go into all that?" Lucy Armanson pleaded. "The last time you told me what was in my corned beef on rye, I couldn't eat it." Lucy pushed her curly black hair back and smiled to take the sting out of her words. "You've got to remember that not everybody has a cast-iron stomach like you."

"She'll need it in medical school," Jennifer said seriously. "All that *blood*."

"I wish you were coming with me," Nora said wistfully. "We could breeze right through those chemistry courses together."

"No thanks," Jennifer said firmly. "The closest I want to get to medical school is our biology lab. Blood turns me off."

"Yuck, how boring," Tracy muttered. Her small rosebud mouth formed a pout. "Will you meet any cute boys in medical school?" Tracy asked.

"Is that all you ever think about — meeting boys?" Susan Hillard asked with a world-weary sigh. She stood up and slammed her milk container on her tray. "Believe it or not, some of us have other things on our minds, Tracy. See you in French, Nora." She flashed the group a brittle smile and stalked away.

There was a moment of embarrassed silence. "Why does she always have it in for me?" Tracy asked plaintively. "Everything I say rubs her the wrong way."

"A lot of people rub Susan the wrong way," Jennifer offered, her hazel eyes warm with sympathy.

"Yeah, tell me about it," Lucy Armanson said and looked at Tracy. She flashed a big grin. "I can ruin her day just by sitting next to her! She's one nasty girl."

Everyone started talking about courses and teachers then, but Nora tuned out, wrapped up in her own thoughts. She thought for the millionth time how lucky she was to have Jennifer Mann as her best friend. Jen happened to look up just then, and their eyes locked briefly across the table.

Nora looked at Jen's pink-and-white skin and black hair and felt a rush of affection for her. It's been this way ever since kindergarten. She knows what I'm going to say before I say it, and sometimes I even finish her sentences for her. We like the same books and movies, we borrow each other's clothes. We could be twins. Sometimes I even think we can read each other's minds.

Chapter 2

"Well, what do you think?" Nora asked as she slammed her locker door shut later that afternoon. "Is this going to be a fantastic year, or what?" Without waiting for an answer, she hugged her books to her chest and flattened herself against the wall, as a group of cheerleaders rushed past her.

Jennifer Mann looked thoughtful. "You can tell all that from one day?"

"Sure," Nora said in a shocked tone. "Can't you?"

"You know I don't make snap judgments the way you do," Jen said gently. She took a bumper sticker out of her shoulder bag and carefully plastered it across the front of her locker door.

"Save the Whales?" Nora read aloud. "I thought we did that last year."

"No, we have to start fighting all over again," Jennifer broke in enthusiastically.

13

"You see, some of the countries refused to sign the agreement to protect the whales, and there's been a problem with the fishing companies, too, and I can give you — "

"Stop! I'm sure you can," Nora said, groaning inwardly. Jen always had a pet cause going. She'd take care of the whole world if she had a chance.

Once a month, Jennifer baked cookies for the Cedar Groves Nursing Home, and stayed to pour cider and chat with the residents. The elderly people there loved the tall, slim, dark-haired girl with the sparkling hazel eyes and the sunny smile.

Kids loved her, too. She helped put on puppet shows at the local orphanage. And every Saturday afternoon, Jen did volunteer work at the animal shelter.

Jennifer took a deep breath and was all set to launch into a speech about the whales when Nora raised her hand pleadingly. "Please, tell me about it on the way home — this place is hazardous to my health!"

They ducked as Jason Anthony zigzagged by on a battered skateboard. It was strictly against school rules, but Jason was a law unto himself. Mr. Robards, the history teacher, once said that if you added up all the demerits against Jason, he'd probably be in detention for the next hundred years. Not a bad idea, Nora thought.

"You want to stop by my house for a while?" Jennifer offered. "I've got some of that almond delight tea you like."

"You're on," Nora said enthusiastically, and linked her arm through Jen's.

When they walked into Jennifer's sparkling blue and white kitchen half an hour later, Nora felt completely at home. The Manns' house *was* a second home to her. She was helping herself to a granola bar out of a Morris cookie jar, when Jeff Crawford wandered into the kitchen.

"Be careful where you walk," he shouted. "I just waxed the floor." He peered at the gleaming tiles. "It's a work of art, if I do say so myself."

A lot of people thought it was really odd that Jen's family had a male housekeeper. Jennifer's mother had died when Jen and her younger brother Eric were practically babies. After that, the Manns' had had a succession of housekeepers, but most of them just thought of the arrangement as a "job."

Jeff was different. He was in his early fifties, with graying hair and bright blue eyes, and he was part of the family.

"We'll try not to walk on your precious floor," Jennifer said, pretending annoyance. "We'll just swing from the chandelier."

"Very funny," he said, taking a swipe at her with a dust rag. "I don't know why I stay here. As you can see, my work is totally unappreciated."

"I *do* appreciate you, Jeff," Jen assured him with warmth. She took a bite out of the granola bar and closed her eyes. "These are sensational. *You* are sensational."

"I've been experimenting with the recipe. It's the wheat germ that gives it the nutty taste," he said seriously. "And you need blackstrap molasses — "

"A great source of iron," Nora said automatically.

"Enough!" Jennifer turned from the stove and waved a potholder at them. "I'm sick of hearing about health foods. Don't you ever feel like pigging out on a Twinkie or a Devil Dog?"

Jeff and Nora exchanged a look. "Never," they said in unison, and then laughed.

Nora stopped suddenly. "Jeff, it's none of my business, but why are you wearing a sweater in this weather? It must be seventy degrees out. Not that it isn't great-looking," she added quickly, taking in the nubby camel-colored wool. "In fact, it looks like it's hand-knit."

Jeff flushed. He ran his finger around the neckline of the sweater. "I admit it's a little warm, but Debby is coming over later, and she wanted me to . . . uh . . . model it for her." He pretended to be very busy stirring honey into his tea.

"Debby Kincaid?" Jennifer squealed, grinning from ear to ear. "Did Debby knit that for you?"

"She did," Jeff said, the blush spreading over his face. "Nice of her, wasn't it?"

"Nice?" Jennifer repeated. "I'd say it sounds serious!" She was about to say more, but the phone rang just then, and Jeff beat a hasty retreat upstairs. "It's for me," he explained.

Nora and Jennifer were silent for a minute, each thinking her own thoughts. "Do you think we'll ever knit sweaters for guys?" Jennifer asked seriously.

"Knit a sweater? You've got to be kidding!" Nora insisted. "Remember last year when we had to donate a homemade craft for the Christmas bazaar? I started out making a macrame wall hanging way back in September, and by December it was only the size of a bookmark!"

"You've told me that three times," Jen said.

"Well, it's the truth. . . ." Nora paused. "I think this year I'll bake a couple of loaves of my famous zucchini bread."

"You mean well, Nora, but you don't

bake any better than you do macrame."

Every time Denise Hendrix walked up the gray flagstone steps to the rambling three-story stone house, she felt a jolt of surprise. It was a beautiful house. The choicest property in town, the real estate agent had said. Then what was wrong with it? It looks like something out of a Hollywood set, she thought, irritated.

She sighed and let herself in the back door. Her mother was talking on the phone, and smilingly pointed to a chocolate chip cake on the cherrywood table.

"Another dinner party," her mother said, as she replaced the receiver and made a note on the kitchen calendar. "Can you believe it? We're already booked up until mid-November! I'd like to return some of these invitations, but it's going to take me weeks to get this place in order."

"That's nice," Denise murmured.

She realized her mother was looking at her in a peculiar way and forced herself to smile and look interested. "I'm sorry, Mom, did you say something?"

"Well, you're certainly in a world of your own, honey," she said, her gray eyes concerned. "How did school go today?"

Denise hesitated. She hated to sound like a complainer. "It was . . . well . . . pretty much what I expected," she hedged.

"Oh, that's good," her mother said cheerfully. "Tony said he's already found some friends. In fact, he's out playing basketball with them right now." She paused. "How about you — did you meet some nice girls?"

Denise bit her lip. She didn't want to lie, but there was no sense in upsetting her mother by telling her the whole truth. "There seem to be quite a few nice girls in my classes."

Why let her mother know she sat at lunch alone? Or that she lost her locker combination and was late for every class because she couldn't figure out her computer cards. Or that she had never felt so alone, and so hopelessly out of it in her life! Give it a chance, she said sternly to herself. Maybe Tony was right. Maybe by some miracle, everything would fall into place.

"I suppose it's going to be a change for you," her mother was saying sympathetically. "Going to a place like Cedar Groves after being at Chateau Remy."

A change! Denise felt like shouting. It's going to be a disaster! "It'll be different," she said, hoping she could keep the panic out of her voice.

Her mother reached across the table then, and patted Denise's hand encouragingly. "Well, just hang in there, honey. I know you're going to love it here. Things have a way of working out for the best, you know."

Denise nodded, and wondered if there was some way she could tactfully escape to her room. Her mother was the most optimistic person she knew, but sometimes her sunny disposition was too much to take. Especially on a day like today.

This was going to be the worst year of her life — she could tell. Coming to the States had been a gigantic mistake. The irony was that she was the only one who seemed to think so. The rest of her family seemed thrilled by the move. And why shouldn't they be? she thought bitterly. Her mother had a new house to decorate, her father had a new business to run, her brother Tony had already acquired a pack of new friends . . . and where did that leave her?

"Nowhere," she said to herself. "Absolutely nowhere."

It was a little past eight-thirty that night when Nora Ryan called Jennifer Mann. There was no real reason to call her, of course. After all, they had just spent the whole day together, and had gone over every detail of their classes, their teachers, their homework, and their wardrobe. They had even discussed Denise Hendrix. "The makeup queen," as Susan Hillard had nastily called her.

But they called each other every night.

"What are you up to?" Nora's standard greeting unleashed a torrent of words and giggles.

"Well, you're not going to believe this," Jen confided, "but I just painted my nails Burgundy Ice. First I used a base coat, then the color, and then a frosted sealer."

"It must have taken forever," Nora said.

"It did. I painted all twenty of them!"

"Fingers?"

"And toes, idiot." Jen paused and lowered her voice. "I was planning to wear open-toed shoes to school tomorrow, and I thought painted toenails would look great. What do you think?"

Nora debated the matter silently. "What else are you going to wear tomorrow?"

"My gray denim jumpsuit with a red leather belt," Jen said promptly.

"Then I'll wear my white cotton jumpsuit," Nora said eagerly. "This will probably be the last time I get to wear it before spring. My mother says you're not supposed to wear white after Labor Day."

"Jeff has a theory about clothes," Jennifer said thoughtfully. "He thinks you should just forget about the season and wear whatever you want. Although, what does he know about clothes? He wears wool sweaters in September."

"True. And all for the love of Debby," Nora agreed. "Do you think there's anything really serious going on there?" she asked after a moment.

"I don't know." Jen's voice sounded small and a little scared. "I think it's great that he met someone like her, but Nora, what will we do if . . . you know?"

"If he moves out," Nora finished the sentence for her. There was a long silence while the two friends pondered this possibility. "Well, the thing to do," Nora said finally, "is not even *think* of that. Everything will work out fine."

My friend, the optimist, Jen thought to herself. "I hope so," she sighed. She lay back on the white chenille bedspread, and stared at her reflection in the long mirror that hung over the dresser. Maybe Nora's right, she admitted. It's silly to get upset, just because Jeff has a girl friend.

Jennifer breathed a sigh of relief. Luckily she had a good friend like Nora to put everything in perspective. "You know what? I always feel a hundred percent better after talking to you."

"You know what? I do, too!"

After they hung up, Jennifer reached

under the bed and pulled out a blue leather diary. She grabbed a pen and settled back on the pillows.

Dear Diary, she wrote. *Today Nora and I are officially eighth-graders. Nora was thrilled and acted like it was a real turning point in her life! I can't say I feel the same. I don't really feel any different, or any more grown-up than I did last year.*

Most of the kids seem like they haven't changed much over the summer. Tracy is just as boy-crazy as ever, and Susan Hillard still doesn't miss a chance to put someone down. She made a couple of cracks to Lucy Armanson today, but Lucy is even quicker at one-liners than Susan is, and it was a stand-off!

There's a new girl named Denise Hendrix, and she's the most beautiful girl I've ever seen (in real life). None of the girls like her — they think she's a snob because she doesn't talk to anyone. So she seems stuck-up. But it could be that she's just shy. I'll let you know more tomorrow. . . .

Your friend, Jennifer.

Chapter 3

It was raining the next morning when Nora's alarm went off, and she lay in bed for a few minutes, listening to the gentle hammering on the roof. She huddled under the covers, then swung her legs gingerly over the edge of the bed, and padded to the closet. The white cotton jumpsuit she had chosen the night before would look dumb in the rain, she decided. She thumbed through her clothes quickly, and finally picked out a pair of khaki jeans and a ruffly white blouse. Not really right for her short, compact body, but it would do.

When she walked into the kitchen, her sister Sally was standing by the window doing leg exercises. She was using the windowsill for a ballet barre, and was swinging her head down to her knee in a graceful arc. From time to time, she'd glance at a biology book on the kitchen table. Sally was a freshman at a nearby university, and made no secret of the fact that she was marking time until she could head for New York to pursue her real dream — professional dancing.

"Nora — thank goodness you're up!" she said feelingly. She dropped her leg to the floor, and quickly cleared a place at the table for Nora. "Sit down, sit down, I've got a million questions I want to ask you."

"Not another bio quiz," Nora sighed. She poured herself a glass of orange juice and stared out the kitchen window at the dark sky. "Honestly, Sally, why don't you study for your tests ahead of time?"

"You sound like my teacher," Sally snapped. Then her face softened. "Look, I'm sorry, Nora. Just help me this once, and I'll make it up to you."

"Hmmm," Nora said doubtfully, and reached for the metal tin of granola. She was very proud of her homemade granola, and made a batch every couple of weeks. Her father always kidded her that if he were stranded on a desert island, he could probably live for twenty or thirty years or so just on Nora's granola.

"Okay," Nora relented. "I'll help. I'll help." For the next ten minutes, Nora took Sally through the major steps in cell construction. Then a horn blared outside.

"That's my ride," Sally said breathlessly. She scooped up her books and then leaned over and gave Nora a quick hug. "Thanks. It's great to have a doctor in the family!"

Nora's mother, Jessica, burst into the kitchen just as the door slammed. "Did Sally leave?" she asked. She poured herself a cup of scalding coffee and started to drink it standing up.

"Just a second ago," Nora said. She stared at her mother in amazement. "You must have an asbestos throat," she said, watching her gulp the coffee.

"I'm just in a mad rush today," her mother said with a smile. "We go to court on the Howard case I told you about." Jessica Ryan was an attorney with the Legal Aid Society, and spent most of her evenings poring over law books.

"How are things at school? I suppose it was fun to see the old crowd again," Mrs. Ryan said.

"It was." For some reason, a girl with shimmering blonde hair popped into her head. "We've got a new student, Mom. A girl from Switzerland. Her name is Denise Hendrix, and she's just moved here with — "

"Did you say Hendrix? That's the cosmetics family!" her mother said in surprise. "I heard they had a daughter about your age," she began, "but I thought she'd be in private school. She looked very pretty in the newspaper picture."

"Denise was in the newspaper?"

"Her family was featured in the business section. I bet their phone hasn't stopped ringing since." She laughed. "Every lawyer and accountant in town wants to do business with them." She glanced at her watch and made a face. "You better hurry or you'll miss your bus!" She rinsed out her cup, blew Nora a kiss, and dashed out the door.

Nora looked at the kitchen clock and panicked. All those lazy summer mornings had spoiled her. She grabbed a handful of granola and picked up her books. She had exactly four minutes to sprint to the bus stop.

"I'm telling you, Denise Hendrix is stuck-up," Susan Hillard said firmly, her thin face pinched into a frown. Susan enjoyed picking at people's weak points, and as far back as Nora could remember, had never said anything good about anyone. "She sits right behind me in algebra, and she never says a word. She's practically a mute!"

"Maybe she doesn't speak English. Somebody said she was from Switzerland," Mia

Stevens offered. Mia was Cedar Groves' resident punk rocker and was decked out on this gray September morning in a tight leather skirt and a dozen plastic bracelets. Her tawny hair was dyed a startling shade of orange, and her eyes were rimmed with heavy charcoal eyeliner.

"She *lived* in Switzerland, she's not *from* there," Nora said patiently. She shifted her books to her other arm and wished the bell would ring. Eighth-graders always congregated on the steps before school every day. It was a tradition. Anyone who went inside before the bell rang would immediately be branded "uncool," or worse.

The bell rang then, just as Jennifer raced up the front steps and collided with her. She was wearing a yellow slicker raincoat with a hood that made her look about eight years old. She caught Nora staring at the raincoat and made a face.

"*Don't* say it!" she said grimly. "Dad went shopping last night, and *this* is what he brought home."

"It's not so bad," Nora said, trying to be reassuring. "Maybe you can start a new trend." Secretly, her heart went out to her friend. Whenever Mr. Mann tried to play mother and father, the results were disastrous.

"Hey, where did you get this?" Mia said,

interested. She plucked the hem of the raincoat with a long magenta fingernail.

"My father picked it up," Jen said defensively.

"Not bad," Mia said.

"Really?" Jennifer looked surprised.

"Well, *not* the way you're wearing it," Mia said, tossing a strand of bleached hair out of her eyes. "But plastic is really *in*, you know." She stepped back and took a long look. "What I'd do is get rid of the hood, push up the sleeves, add a belt, and you've got a minidress."

Nora and Jennifer exchanged a look. "Now there's an idea," Nora said, trying to keep a straight face.

The second bell rang then, and Nora and Jen joined the crowd that was pushing its way through the heavy double doors into the main corridor. They had homeroom together and minutes later were settled in room 332, under the watchful eye of Mr. Mario. Mr. Mario looked both bored and irritated, Nora noticed, which meant they would have a long year ahead of them.

"I hope everybody has taken the same seats they took yesterday," he droned in a monotone. He was a tired-looking man, with thinning brown hair that he brushed carefully across his forehead.

He stopped as the door opened and a girl

in a shocking pink slicker and plum stirrup pants appeared. A blonde girl who had eyes as clear and blue as Lake Geneva, Jennifer thought. If Lake Geneva was blue.

"And who are *you*?" Mr. Mario asked, annoyed. "The bell has already rung."

"I'm . . . Denise Hendrix," the girl said haltingly. Someone in the back of the room gave a low wolf whistle, and Denise flushed.

"Well, take your seat," Mr. Mario ordered, and pulled out a pair of thick reading glasses.

Denise looked helplessly around the crowded homeroom.

"Right here, Denise," Tommy Ryder offered. He patted his chair invitingly. "Best seat in the house." Tommy leaned back in his chair, laughing hysterically at his own joke. Nora looked at him coldly. He was good-looking, she had to admit, with sandy brown hair and a wide flashing smile, but impossibly conceited. Tommy was convinced that every girl in the eighth grade was ready to fall at his feet, and to Nora's disgust, some of them were.

"Where . . . uh, should I sit?" Denise asked timidly. Her voice was clear and sweet.

Mr. Mario pushed his glasses up on his forehead and peered at her with a thin-lipped smile. "Where you sat *yesterday*," he said in a long-suffering tone.

"But I didn't *have* a seat yesterday," she said, more forcefully. "I wasn't here yesterday."

"And where were you, may I ask?" His voice was tinged with sarcasm.

Denise looked as though she wished she could melt into the floor. "I went to the wrong homeroom," she said tremulously. Her lower lip quivered, and Jennifer wondered for one awful moment if she was going to cry. When Mr. Mario continued to stare at her, she made a helpless little gesture with her hands. "I'm not used to these computer cards and — " she waved a stack of them, and the whole pile fluttered to the floor " — oh, no!" she wailed.

There was an immediate scramble as half a dozen boys rushed to pick up the cards. "Have no fear!" Tommy Ryder said loudly. "It's Ryder to the rescue!" He snatched a card away from Mitch Pauley, who immediately snatched it back.

"Hey, I saw it first!" Mitch objected. There was a brief tussle and one of the cards was ripped in half.

"Stop it immediately!" Mr. Mario's voice boomed through the room. "This is a classroom, not a football scrimmage." He glared at Mitch and Tommy. "Give the young lady her cards and then take your seats."

There was dead silence as the boys sheepishly handed the cards to Denise. She ignored the broad wink that Tommy Ryder gave her, and desperately tried to put them in order.

"Now, let's start over." Mr. Mario gave a martyr's smile and held out his hand. "Do you have one that says Mario on it?" he said with heavy patience.

"Uh, yes, I think so." Denise gulped. She handed him the card and tried to ignore the twenty-five pairs of eyes riveted on her. The room was impossibly still.

"Denise Hendrix," Mr. Mario said. He read the name and then peered at her as if she were an imposter. "You're a transfer," he said accusingly. "You should have told me."

"I'm sorry," she said automatically. She could feel the color race to her cheeks and her mouth felt suddenly dry. I can't seem to do anything right in this place, she thought miserably.

"Take this back to the office, get a T-admit slip, and come back here tomorrow morning. On time," he said warningly.

"A T-admit slip?"

"Transfer admit — they know what it is," he added curtly.

The bell rang then and Denise was propelled out the door by a surge of bodies.

Jennifer fought her way through the crowd and caught up with her in the hall.

"Here's one of the cards they missed," she said, touching Denise on the elbow.

Denise whirled around as if someone were attacking her, and then her face relaxed. "Oh, thanks," she said and tucked the card into her notebook. She would have liked to say something else, but a red-haired boy with freckles elbowed his way next to her.

"*Parlez-vous français?*" he asked, leering into her face.

"Idiot," she said softly under her breath and swept away.

Jason Anthony turned to see Jennifer staring at him. A huge grin spread over his face and he jabbed his thumb toward the departing Denise. "She's crazy about me," he said, leaning close to Jennifer. "I can always tell!"

Denise made her way resolutely down the hall. Her second day at Cedar Groves, and it had been a . . . what was that expression they used? A bummer.

She glanced at the schedule she had crumpled up in her hand and saw that she had a free period. This would be a good time to go to the office and get that slip Mr. Mario had asked for. But where was the office? It was so easy to get turned around in this place! She was about to retrace her steps when two boys fell into place beside her.

"We'll save a seat for you in homeroom tomorrow," Tommy Ryder said, nudging a tall, athletic-looking boy, who laughed on cue. "Isn't that right, Mitch?"

"Absolutely," Mitch Pauley said, turning the full force of his brown eyes on her. Mitch was the captain of the Cedar Groves Junior High football team and had been voted best all-around athlete in the school. He smiled at Denise, confident that she would giggle and be impressed the way a lot of the girls were. Maybe she'd like to see him play in the first home game, he thought, looking at her from the corner of his eye. He'd have to edge out Tommy Ryder, of course, but that shouldn't be any problem. Not once Denise found out who *he* was. He was glad he'd worn his letter sweater today. He was sure she'd ask him about it.

"You sure are quiet," Tommy was saying to her.

"Maybe Swedish girls don't talk much," Mitch offered helpfully. He eyed her long blonde hair that fell in silky waves to her shoulders. "They sure have pretty hair, though."

"I'm from Switzerland, not Sweden," Denise said tightly. What a jerk! she thought angrily.

Tommy laughed. "You've got to excuse Mitch. He's not really up on his geography." He edged a little closer to her, and quickened his steps to match hers. "He's a jock, you know," he said in a low voice. "Great guy, but. . . ." He tapped his head meaningfully.

"Hey, what are you telling her?" Mitch said suspiciously, bringing up the rear.

Tommy grinned, managing to show his dazzling white teeth. "Oh, I was saying that I was kind of the academic type, myself."

"The academic type?" Mitch snorted. "You've got to be kidding! The only thing you'd get an A in would be girl-watching."

The bell rang just as Denise spotted the office. She sprinted forward, taking the two boys by surprise.

"Hey, we'll see you at lunch," Tommy called as she disappeared through the double glass door. When she didn't answer, he shrugged and turned to Mitch. "If I didn't know better, I'd think I was losing my touch," he said a little nervously.

Chapter 4

"But there's no point in my taking French," Denise was explaining to Mrs. Peters in the office. "You see, I already speak it fluently."

Mrs. Peters raised a skeptical eyebrow and Denise felt the color rise to her cheeks. "I've lived in Switzerland for the past five years," she said, struggling to keep her voice steady.

Mrs. Peters finally raised her head from a stack of computer cards and stared at a point somewhere over Denise's left shoulder. "You know you have to fulfill a two-year language requirement for graduation," she said in a flat voice. She patted her tightly curled gray hair and looked meaningfully at the clock. "I hope you realize you should be in class right now, young lady," she said with a thin smile.

"Unless you feel like chalking up a demerit."

"What?" Denise said, startled. That's all she needed. A demerit on the second day of school. "No, there must be some mistake, I'm positive I've got a free period now." She snatched the computer cards off the counter and flipped through them desperately. "Look, it says free period right here," she said triumphantly. "See? Eight to nine on Mondays."

"Read the bottom of the card," Mrs. Peters said, barely moving her lips.

Denise's eyes raced down the card and her spirits sank. There it was, printed in block capitals: STUDENTS ARE REQUIRED TO REPORT TO ASSIGNED STUDY HALLS DURING FREE PERIOD UNLESS EXCUSED WITH AN X-SLIP FROM THE OFFICE.

X-slips . . . T-slips . . . Denise thought sinkingly. Was there no end to it?

"I didn't realize," she said numbly. "What should I do?"

"Report to your study hall immediately," Mrs. Peters said crisply. "The room number is stamped on the right-hand top corner of your schedule sheet."

Denise turned to go and then stopped. Taking a deep breath, she began, "About that French class. . . ."

"You can take another language instead," the woman replied. She consulted a computer screen and handed Denise a punch card. "There's one opening left in Mr. Mario's class."

It wasn't until Denise was in the hall that it dawned on her. Oh, no, not Mr. Mario, her homeroom teacher! She glanced at the card and her heart sank. MARIO, SALVATORE. BEGINNING ITALIAN, MONDAY-FRIDAY. That meant she'd be seeing Mr. Mario every single day for the next semester, first in homeroom, and then in class. "Me and my big mouth," she muttered under her breath.

"I don't know why we have to take cooking," Nora said plaintively a couple of hours later. "I think it's really unfair. After all, I'm not going to spend my life in the kitchen — I'm going to be a doctor."

"Nora, even doctors have to eat," Jennifer retorted. "You can't live on banana chips and hazlenuts forever." She reached under the counter and pulled out a heavy stainless steel pot. The class was making vegetable soup that day, and she and Nora were in charge of chopping up potatoes and carrots.

"Well, I feel like I'm on KP duty," Nora complained.

"Just tell yourself that it's better than

shop," Jennifer said practically. "Next semester we get to take drafting or small-engine repair."

She began peeling carrots and laying them side by side on a giant wooden chopping block. She didn't mind taking home ec class as much as Nora did. In fact she liked the idea of learning how to cook for a large group of people.

"Hey, who's got the parsley?" Steve Crowley shouted from a neighboring counter. Steve was a tall boy with dark brown hair and blue eyes. He wore a red-and-white apron with VALENTINE'S plastered across it. "One of the advantages of having a father in the restaurant business," he joked.

"I think it's in that little white box in the spice rack," Nora told him.

"Parsley in a box?" He clutched his chest and staggered backward as if he had been shot. "My father would die — right on the spot."

"What's the problem?" Tracy asked innocently. She looked up into his face, smiling. Why does he play so hard to get? she wondered. She'd been trying to get Steve to notice her ever since seventh grade, but he acted like she was invisible.

"Parsley is supposed to be fresh," he said with conviction. "You should have a pot of it growing on the windowsill."

"Steve," Miss Morton laughed, "this is not the kitchen of a fancy restaurant." Cedar Groves was Miss Morton's first teaching assignment, and she looked so young that a lot of students mistook her for a senior.

The rest of the hour passed quickly, and Nora and Jen were filing out the door when Tracy edged over to them.

"He's so cute," she said dreamily.

"Who?" Jennifer asked curiously.

"Steve Crowley, silly."

Jennifer and Nora exchanged a look and Tracy flushed. "Well, look, I mean . . . don't you guys think he's cute?"

Nora laughed. "We've known him practically forever — "

"Since kindergarten," Jennifer interrupted.

"What does that have to do with it?" Tracy demanded.

"Nothing," Nora said quickly. "It's just that. . . ." She paused and wondered how to explain it. The idea of Steve Crowley being cute or not cute seemed ridiculous. He was their friend, their buddy.

"Don't either one of you guys ever think about dating him?" Tracy said. "You certainly have plenty of opportunity. He talks to you enough," she added moodily.

Jennifer looked at her, her hazel eyes cool and serious. "Tracy, we went to kindergarten with Steve."

"So?"

"So you just don't think about dating someone you shared your fingerpaints with!"

The bell rang just then, and Nora and Jennifer dashed off to French, leaving a very puzzled Tracy staring after them.

"Do you think Tracy was serious?" Jennifer whispered a few minutes later. Mr. Armand, the French teacher, was late, and she and Nora were huddled side by side in the last row.

"About Steve? Definitely," Nora said flatly. "She's got a crush on him a mile long. Didn't you see the way she was staring at him in home ec — with those big, dopey eyes like a sick cow?"

"Nora," Jen said hesitantly, "do you think we'll ever. . . ." She let her voice trail off and took a quick glance around the room. ". . . feel that way about anyone?"

Nora stared at her. "I should hope not!" she whispered fiercely. "Jen, if you ever catch me making an idiot of myself over a boy the way Tracy does, I want you to do me a favor."

"A favor?" Jen asked, surprised.

"I want you to give me a good swift kick." Nora paused. "Not that I feel the urge coming on, but I want you to remember to, just in case."

"I'll remember," Jen promised. She ducked as a paper airplane skidded across the desk, and then looked up to see Tommy Ryder's smirking face.

"Creep," Nora said softly, and shot the airplane back at him. "A case of arrested development," she added smugly. She had read that phrase in her sister Sally's psychology textbook and liked it. "Half the boys in eighth grade act like babies."

"And the other half?" Jen teased her.

Nora shrugged. "A few of them are okay. As friends," she added hastily.

"I suppose we'll want to start dating soon," Jennifer said thoughtfully, after a moment. "If you had to pick out somebody to date, who would it be?" she asked.

"Somebody here in class?" Nora wrinkled her nose. "Gosh," Nora said slowly, "I wouldn't know where to start. I know I wouldn't pick Tommy Ryder," she said feelingly, as another airplane found its target. "Or Mitch Pauley," she added as she recognized his irritating laugh. She turned and glared at him. "Some date he'd make! He'd talk about football scores all night."

"What *do* people talk about on dates?" Jennifer wondered. "I wouldn't know what to say, would you?"

"Sally used to make a list of conversation topics and memorize it," Nora said solemnly.

"You're kidding!" Jennifer's hazel eyes widened, and she twisted a lock of black hair around her finger.

"No, it's the truth. She'd write down all the funny things that happened to her during the week, and then she'd tape it to her mirror and memorize it while she was getting ready to go out."

"Gosh," Jennifer said, awed. She wanted to ask more, but Mr. Armand strode noisily into class just then, and began writing verb conjugations on the blackboard. Jennifer dutifully began copying them in her notebook, but she couldn't take her mind off Sally and her list. What if nothing funny ever happened to you all week? Should you postpone your date, or take a chance and go anyway? Or what if *you* thought the things on the list were funny, but your boyfriend didn't? Should you make up a new list — or find a new boyfriend? The whole thing was very complicated, she decided.

"Twenty-four right, thirty left, and fifteen right," Denise muttered under her breath. Or is it thirty right and twenty-four left? she wondered. She gave the combination lock a furious spin and then yanked on the door. Nothing happened. Who had invented these monsters? she asked herself, giving the door a sharp kick.

She glanced down the hall and frowned. The crazy thing was, nobody else seemed to be having any trouble with their lockers. Dozens of kids were cheerfully stashing books and papers and twirling the locks like it was the easiest thing in the world to do. The locker next to hers flew open, and Denise caught a glimpse of a Duran Duran poster. Unbelievable! she thought. She couldn't even get *into* her locker, and other kids were *decorating* theirs!

And then, by some miracle, the door creaked open, and Denise gasped in surprise. She had actually done it! And with any luck, she'd only be a few minutes late for history class. She grabbed the battered textbook from the top shelf of her locker and slammed the door shut as the bell sounded. She glanced at the map of the school she had taped inside her notebook. "Room 108, corridor C, lower level. That shouldn't be too hard to find," she said to herself. She'd be late, but not by much.

Surely no one would quibble over a few minutes.

"Do you always like to make a grand entrance, Miss Hendrix?" Mr. Carpenter said five minutes later in icy tones.

"No, of course not, I. . . ." she began, and her mind went blank. What could she say? Whatever she said seemed to put her in the wrong.

"I don't like being late," she finished lamely. There was a snicker from someone sitting near the window, and she recognized the boy who had teased her in Mr. Mario's class. Tommy something. When it looked like Mr. Carpenter was going to glare at her forever, she decided to speak up. "You see, I had trouble with my locker," she said, easing herself into an empty seat.

"Trouble with your locker," Mr. Carpenter repeated thoughtfully, stroking his beard. There was another round of titters as she sat down, and Denise could feel herself flushing. Why wouldn't they just let her alone! She shot a furious look at Tommy Ryder.

Mr. Carpenter ordered everyone to turn to page thirty-three, and Denise flipped open her book. She stared blankly at the page. What were quadratic equations doing in the middle of a history textbook?

Then it dawned on her. She had left her history book in her locker.

"Oh, no," she moaned softly, just as Mr. Carpenter called on her to read the first paragraph. "My book is back in my locker," she said, wanting to bury her face in her hands.

"Your book is back in your locker." The room was very still. "Then I would suggest, Miss Hendrix, that you get it!" His voice rose to a crescendo on the last words, but it didn't matter, because Denise was already out of her seat and bolting toward the door.

"Yes, sir," she cried, flying down the aisle.

She didn't stop running till she got all the way back to her locker and then she leaned against the wall to catch her breath. At least she knew the combination now, she thought gratefully. She'd simply get the book, go back to class, and. . . . She stared at her locker door and felt like someone had kicked her in the stomach. She bent down and peered at it nervously. There was some awful gooky stuff stuck all over it . . . something pink and sticky . . . something like . . . bubble gum! Somebody had jammed her locker with bubble gum!

She gave a little cry and darted blindly down the hall.

Chapter 5

"Hendrix?" The phys. ed. teacher's voice bounced around the walls of the drafty gymnasium.

"She's not here," Susan Hillard replied with a sly smile. She took a quick look over her shoulder at the ragged line of girls in identical white blouses and navy blue shorts. No gleaming blonde head appeared. You could always tell when Denise was in a room, she thought disgustedly. Nobody at Cedar Groves — nobody in the whole world, probably — had hair like that.

"Does anybody know where Hendrix is?" Mrs. Scott asked, her pencil poised over her clipboard.

"Probably back in the Alps," Susan muttered, and got a giggle from the girls in the front row.

"Well, if any of you see her, would you please remind her she's already missed two classes. If she's absent one more time, I'm

47

going to have to fail her." She finished the rest of the roll call, and slid back a heavy plywood panel to reveal a long horizontal mirror. "Our gift from the principal," she explained. "Now you girls can watch yourselves as you do aerobics — I want to see some real effort today!"

"Wonderful," Nora muttered. She wasn't a bit like her sister Sally when it came to exercise, and dreaded the daily workouts. Jennifer, on the other hand, seemed to blossom when the pulsating sounds of rock music filled the gym. Nora glanced over at her friend and smiled. Her dark hair was flying, and her eyes were serious and intense as she moved gracefully through the warm-up.

Meanwhile, two floors away, Denise stood in the center corridor, puzzled. She was late for . . . phys. ed., she decided, squinting at her schedule. There it was, phys. ed. West Gym, 1:00-2:00. She was more confused than ever. West Gym? Were there two? And which way was west? She frowned and bit her lip. There was no one she could ask. Absolutely no one. She took a few tentative steps down the hall and saw Mrs. Peters staring suspiciously at her through the glass office wall. She supposed she could go in the office and ask directions, but she decided against it. She'd be darned if she would give the woman the satisfaction of knowing she was lost again!

She turned her notebook sideways and looked at the map. If only she could figure out which way was west! She stood hesitating for a moment, and then she saw something out of the corner of her eye that spurred her to action: Mrs. Peters had gotten to her feet and was making her way steadily around the desk toward the office door. She's probably all set to give me a demerit for loitering in the hall, Denise thought. Clutching the map, she made a sharp right turn, and set off at a jog down the corridor. Please let this be west, she breathed. She made a few more sharp right turns and found herself in a totally unfamiliar part of the school. It seemed older and more rundown — if that was possible — and the grimy walls were covered with grafitti. She was about to retrace her steps when she heard the familiar thump of a volleyball hitting a wooden floor. She had found her way to the gym! She couldn't believe her luck.

With a sigh of relief, she pulled open a heavy metal door and rushed into the room. She was instantly aware that she had made a mistake. A major, horrible mistake! She had found the gym, but she had also found herself right smack in the middle of a *boys'* volleyball game! Fifteen boys stopped to stare at her, as the teacher blew the whistle.

"Hey, Denise, you can play on my team anytime!" someone shouted.

"No, I saw her first!" a boy with a toothy grin yelled. It seemed like the whole room was filled with laughing faces, and Denise backed helplessly toward the door.

"Play ball!" the teacher ordered, glaring at Denise. "And you — " he said, pointing his finger at her " — out!"

She threw open the door and started to charge through when she caught a glimpse of a boy with a towel over his head. A boy with a towel? She wasn't in the hall. She was in the boys' locker room. She felt like her brain had stalled, and her feet refused to carry her forward. There was another chorus of laughter, and someone hooted, "Wrong door, Denise!"

She slammed the door, and through a haze of tears, she somehow managed to find the right door and stumble into the hall. She'd never live this down! The whole school would be laughing at her. She ran blindly down the hall. She had to find someplace to be alone, she had to find someplace to hide.

"Do you want to stop at Temptations?" Jennifer asked Nora at three o'clock that day. The final bell had just rung, and they were stashing their books in their lockers.

"Sure, if we can split a blueberry yogurt delight," Nora said agreeably.

"Okay," Jennifer laughed. "But only if we can get a double fudge sundae next time."

"You're on!" Nora slammed her locker door and turned to her friend. "Let's make a quick stop in the girls' room, okay? My hands still smell like formaldehyde after biology lab. I don't know what they did to that frog, but — "

"Please, don't say it," Jennifer pleaded. "You know I don't have your strong stomach."

The girls' room was empty and Jennifer fastened her long black hair in barrettes, as Nora scrubbed her hands. Nora was humming softly to herself over the sound of the rushing water, when she suddenly stopped and held up a soapy hand.

"Did you hear that?" she hissed to Jennifer.

"What?" Jennifer stared at Nora in the mirror.

"Shhh!" Nora commanded. "There it is again. Kind of a wailing noise."

"I don't hear anything. It's probably the pipes," Jennifer said. She reached over and turned off the faucets. "See, that's all it was — " She was about to say something else, when a low, snuffling sound made both girls look at each other in surprise.

Jennifer was the first to recover. "Nora," she said softly. "Somebody's in there — " she pointed to a closed lavatory door " — and she's crying!"

They both stood listening helplessly as the noise continued. "What should we do?" Jennifer mouthed.

"There's only one thing to do," Nora said briskly. "Let's find out what's going on." She walked over to the door, and tapped firmly on it. "Are you okay in there?"

The answer was a long, drawn-out sob.

"I said, are you okay?" Nora repeated loudly. "Are you sick or something?"

"Maybe we should get the nurse," Jennifer said worriedly.

"No!" The voice from behind the door was surprisingly clear. And familiar somehow, Jennifer thought. It had a trace of an accent. . . .

"Well, at least we know you're alive," Nora said. "Why don't you come out and tell us what's wrong? Maybe we can — "

"Go away," the voice ordered. There was another long sob, and the sound of someone blowing her nose. "Just go away and mind your own business."

Jennifer was sure she recognized that

voice. "We just want to help you," she spoke up.

"You can't help." Followed by a series of hiccups.

"Look, this is crazy, talking to a door," Nora said. She was starting to get annoyed. Nothing was more frustrating than trying to help someone who didn't want to be helped! She looked at Jennifer and said quietly, "We'll be standing here all day. Let's go."

"No," Jen whispered. "Wait."

Nora took a deep breath. "Wait for what? The girl wants us to go."

Jen considered this for a moment. "There's only one thing to do." She rapped loudly on the door. "I just want you to know that if you're not coming out — we're coming in!"

"No!" The voice rose to a shriek.

"Oh, yes we are!" Jen answered. She handed Nora her books and got down on her hands and knees, hoping she wouldn't ruin her jeans. "I feel pretty silly," she muttered. She ducked her head under the lavatory door and squirmed underneath. When she stood up, she saw Denise Hendrix huddled against the wall. "It's you!" she said, unlocking the door.

"Denise," Nora said, "what in the world is wrong?"

Denise was a pitiful sight. Her eyes were red and puffy from crying and her nose was swollen. Her eye makeup had streaked down her face, and she reminded Jennifer of a sad clown.

"Denise, come on out," Jennifer said, taking her gently by the arm. She led her to the sink and dabbed at her face with a wet tissue.

"I told you, I just want to be alone," Denise said flatly.

"That's good enough for me!" Nora said, and started to turn toward the door. What would Denise Hendrix possibly have to cry about? Probably a broken fingernail, she thought, irritated.

"Nora, wait!" Jennifer pleaded. "We can't leave her here like this."

"No?" Nora said impatiently. "Jen, she doesn't want us!" She had her hand on the door handle, and then a funny thing happened. Denise hiccuped. Nora turned around startled, and then without meaning to, burst out laughing.

"Nora!" Jennifer said, shocked. She couldn't believe her friend would laugh at a time like this.

"I'm sorry," Nora apologized. "It's just that I've never seen anyone hiccup and cry at the same time."

"Well, it happens to me all the time,"

Denise said defensively. She stared at herself in the mirror. "I look a mess," she said in a little voice. Jennifer silently passed her a brush, and Denise began to brush her tousled blonde hair.

"How . . . uh, long have you been in here?" Jennifer asked, curiously.

"Ever since fourth period." She began to fix her eye makeup and started to hiccup again.

"Here, drink this," Nora said in her best doctor tone. "Slowly." She handed her a paper cup of water.

Denise took a sip and made a face. "It tastes awful," she said, wiping her mouth. "The water in Switzerland was pure . . . like a mountain spring," she added softly.

Nora had a sudden idea. "Is that what this is all about? Are you homesick?" she demanded.

Denise looked startled. "Of course I'm homesick, but. . . ."

"But what?" Jennifer said encouragingly. "There's got to be more to it than that." She sat on the tile floor and leaned her back against the wall. "Why don't you sit down and tell us about it?"

Denise gave them a long look, and finally sat down on the floor, with her knees drawn up to her chin. "I don't know where to start," she said helplessly.

"At the beginning," Nora said crisply.

When she didn't answer, Jennifer piped up, "We don't know much about you, Denise. All we really know about you is that you're from Switzerland." And that your family is worth a fortune! she added silently.

"I moved here from Lucerne," Denise began slowly. "And I'm a little older than you are. I'm fourteen." Nora raised her eyebrows, and Denise said quickly, "I missed a year of school because we moved around so much."

She fell silent again, and Jennifer said cheerfully, "I suppose things over here are pretty different for you."

Denise reacted like she'd been shot. "Pretty different? They're . . . they're awful!" And then she burst into tears again and buried her head in her hands.

"You don't like it here?" Jennifer was amazed. She loved everything about Cedar Groves and couldn't imagine wanting to be anywhere else.

Denise raised her head to look at her. "Would you like being in a place where everyone hated you?"

"But Denise," Jennifer said, "no one hates you. Not really."

"Nobody likes me," Denise pointed out.

Jennifer hesitated, and shot a pleading

look at Nora. "You haven't given anyone a chance to know you. You keep pretty much to yourself, you know." Jennifer paused and wondered how far to go. "A lot of the kids think you're a snob," she said gently. Part of the problem is the way you look, she longed to say.

"I'm not a snob," Denise said, her blue eyes blazing. She looked imploringly at the two girls. "You can't imagine what it's been like for me these past few days. How lonely I've been."

Nora stared at her, and wondered if she was telling the truth. After all, if she had just given the Cedar Groves kids a chance, they would have been friendly to her.

"It's bad enough to be in a strange place," Denise went on. "But I've made such a mess of everything here! I'm late for every class because I get lost all the time, and I can't figure out my schedule because it's written on computer cards . . . and someone stuffed gum in my locker today!" She paused and blew her nose.

"Denise," Jennifer said, trying not to smile, "it's not the end of the world, you know. Those sorts of things happen to everybody, not all in one day, of course, but — "

"But the point is not to let them get you down," Nora said.

"You sound just like my mother," Denise said, smiling for the first time. "She's an optimist, too."

"Well, she's right," Jennifer said earnestly. "All you have to do is give the kids here a chance — you'll have dozens of friends!"

"I will?" Denise looked doubtful.

"Of course you will," Jennifer insisted. "And you can start with us. We'll be your friends, won't we, Nora?"

There was dead silence while two pairs of eyes swung toward Nora, who gulped and stammered, "Uh, well . . . sure."

"See, it's all settled," Jennifer said warmly. "You won't have to worry about getting lost anymore, or trying to figure things out by yourself, because you'll have your friends with you." She stood up and extended her hand to Denise. "I think this calls for a celebration, and I know just the place to go. Denise," she said, "how does a double chocolate fudge sundae sound to you?"

"It sounds great," Denise answered, her face brightening. "Can we go somewhere and get one?"

"We sure can," Jennifer said, giving Nora a push toward the door.

Chapter 6

"I can't believe you did that," Nora said. A light rain was falling as she and Jennifer walked home from Temptations, and she jumped to one side to avoid a puddle.

"What?" Jennifer said innocently. Her hazel eyes were amused as she pulled up the hood on her slicker to protect her long, dark hair.

"You *know* what!" Nora rolled her eyes. "You had to open your big mouth and invite Denise to come out for ice cream with us."

"Big deal," Jennifer replied.

"And now she thinks we're her best friends," Nora finished glumly.

Jennifer laughed. "Is that so terrible?" When Nora didn't answer, she went on cheerfully, "I think Denise is really nice. Just think, everybody at school thought she was so stuck-up, and all this time she's been dying to make friends. It really makes you stop and think, doesn't it?"

While Jennifer chatted on happily, Nora shivered in her light jacket and glanced at the darkening sky. It was going to be a bleak, rainy night, and she could hardly wait to get home.

"Sometimes we completely misjudge people," Jennifer was saying feelingly. Nora took one look at her glowing face and dancing eyes and her spirits sank. Nora had seen that look before and she knew exactly what it meant — Jennifer was hot on the trail of a new "project."

"There's no reason we can't be friends with her, is there?" Jennifer was saying earnestly.

"Uh, no, I guess not," Nora said reluctantly. Jennifer would never understand that she still had her doubts about Denise. Denise had been okay at Temptations, she had to admit, but she just wasn't the kind of girl she would ever pick as a friend. She seemed a lot older than the rest of their crowd, for one thing, and it was obvious that they had about as much in common as mustard and ice cream.

"You still don't think she's a snob, do you?" Jennifer persisted.

"No, I think she's probably okay," Nora said grudgingly.

"Good!" Jen answered enthusiastically. "I do, too. The three of us are going to have great times together. I can tell!"

"Sure," Nora said uneasily. She wished Jen would take things a little slower. After all, there was no sense in rushing into this friendship with Denise. The whole problem with Jen, she thought, as she ran up the steps to her front porch, is that she's just too open and too friendly with people.

Later that night, Nora was curled up in bed in her red snuggly pajamas when the phone rang. It's Jen again, she thought, and laid her book down the bedspread.

"Nora?" The voice on the other end of the line was soft and hesitant, with a trace of an accent.

"Denise?" Nora asked, puzzled.

"Yes, it's me," Denise said breathlessly. "I'm sorry to call you so late," she rushed on, "but I just had this fantastic idea, and I wanted to tell you about it. That is, if you're not busy."

"No, go ahead," Nora said, trying to put a note of enthusiasm in her voice. Her eyes stole longingly to her book, and she sighed and laid it on the night table.

"Well, I was thinking about how much fun we had today at Temptations. . . ." Denise paused, and seemed to be waiting for her to say something.

"We sure did," Nora said, trying to be agreeable. "We'll have to do it again sometime." But not too soon, she added silently.

". . . and I thought it would be great if I could get to know some of the other kids, too."

"Hmmm, sounds like a good idea," Nora said, half listening.

"So I decided to have an overnight party, and you and Jen are the very first people on my list!"

It took a moment for it to sink in. Denise was definitely waiting for an answer.

"An overnight party," Nora repeated, stalling for time. "When would it be?" she added, as her mind raced through a string of possible excuses. She could be going out of town, she could be baby-sitting, she could even be sick, if necessary.

"This Friday night," Denise said eagerly. "Can you make it?"

"Uh. . . ." Nora's mind ground to a halt. Jen always said she was a terrible liar. "Sure, I guess so," she mumbled. She sounded hoarse.

"What did you say?"

"I said, sure, I'd love to come." Nora smiled into the phone. Her speech teacher always said that if you want to sound warm and convincing on the phone, you should smile a lot. This seemed like a good time to try it out, and Nora grinned from ear to ear. It must have worked, because Denise gave a cry of joy.

"Great! Look," she said hurriedly, "I'll tell you all the details tomorrow at school, okay? I've got a dozen more people I want to call tonight."

A dozen? "Sure, I'll see you then," Nora told her. The moment Denise hung up, Nora quickly dialed Jennifer's number. She frowned when a busy signal rang in her ear. "Now Denise will get to her first," she muttered.

"Did you get a phone call from Denise last night?" Nora demanded the next morning. They were changing into blouses and shorts for their fourth period gym class with Mrs. Scott.

"Yes, isn't it wonderful?" Jen looked pleased. "She said she'd already invited you to the sleep-over. I was really surprised, weren't you?"

"That's the understatement of the year," Nora muttered, pulling the shapeless navy blue shorts over her hips. "If I had had more time, I could have come up with an excuse."

"An excuse?" Jennifer's eyes widened in surprise. "Why would you want to do that? I think it's really neat of her to invite us," she said staunchly. "I haven't been to a sleep-over in ages."

Nora glanced nervously at the clock. The bell was going to ring in exactly three minutes, and she knew she'd have to scramble to get dressed. Out of the corner of her eye, she could see Mrs. Scott standing in the center of the gym, pencil in hand, ready to take attendance. And all set to hand out tardy slips, Nora thought grimly.

"Just tell me what you've got against her," Jennifer persisted challengingly.

"I don't have anything against her," Nora protested. "It's just that —" She stopped, considering. "Look, we'll talk about it later, okay? You don't want to be late for class, do you?" She pulled Jen through the door, just as Mrs. Scott blew her whistle.

Jennifer quickly scanned the class, but Denise was nowhere in sight. "I hope Denise makes it today," she whispered, as she and Nora took their places in the lineup.

Nora rolled her eyes. "She's got to grow up sometime," she said flatly. As far as she was concerned, the whole thing with Denise was getting out of hand. Going out for ice cream with her was bad enough, but now it looked like Jen was practically ready to *adopt* her!

By some miracle, Mrs. Scott misplaced

her grade book and hunted for it for several minutes, while Jennifer kept her eyes glued on the locker room door. "Hurry up, Denise, hurry *up*," she said under her breath.

Finally, Mrs. Scott found the missing book and called the roll in her best drill-sergeant voice. When she got to the H's, Jennifer held her breath. She didn't dare turn around, but she crossed her fingers and hoped that Denise would appear.

"Harris, Hart, Henderson," the voice droned on, and then suddenly stopped. "Is Hendrix here?"

A moment's pause, and then a soft voice from the back of the room said, "Here!"

Mrs. Scott frowned. "Step forward, Hendrix, I want to talk to you," she said, fingering the whistle she wore around her neck. "You've missed the first two classes and I want to know — " She broke off suddenly as Denise walked timidly to the center of the room. "What are you doing in those clothes?" Mrs. Scott asked in disbelief.

Jennifer couldn't stand the suspense anymore and swung around just as Susan Hillard snickered. "I guess that's what they're wearing in Switzerland this year," she said in a catty voice. She grinned at Jennifer, who glared back at her.

Then Jennifer looked at Denise. "Oh, no," she said softly. Instead of wearing the regulation uniform — a white short-sleeved blouse and baggy blue shorts — Denise was wearing a pair of skin-tight white shorts with a bright pink sweater top. The top was pulled down on one shoulder, *Flashdance*-style, and Denise had knotted a plum calico scarf around her neck. Her trim legs were encased in pink legwarmers and she shifted her weight nervously from one foot to the other.

"What do you mean?" she asked hesitantly.

"You're not dressed," Mrs. Scott said, and someone in the back row giggled.

"I'm not?" Denise looked down at her legwarmers, as if searching for an explanation, and then back up at Mrs. Scott.

"I mean you're not dressed for *gym*!" Mrs. Scott said.

"Oh, I thought — " Denise looked helplessly around the room " — I thought this is what everybody wore," she said falteringly. A pink flush crept up her face and she clenched and unclenched her long slim fingers together behind her back.

"She thinks she's a *Solid Gold* dancer!" Susan hooted.

"That's enough, Hillard," Mrs. Scott said angrily. She reached out and grabbed

Jennifer's arm. "You, Ryan," she commanded, "take her back to the locker room and get her outfitted. You'll find extra shorts and tops in the bottom of the back cupboard." She pressed a key in Jennifer's hand. "On the double," she added. She waited until the two girls scampered off, before turning back to the class. "Now, are we going to stand around, or are we going to play ball?"

"I can't believe I've done it again," Denise moaned, as she and Jen squatted on the floor, sorting through a pile of faded gym clothes. "Mrs. Scott must think I'm the biggest jerk in the world."

"No, she doesn't," Jennifer said sympathetically, and then she giggled. "You certainly got everyone's attention in that outfit, though."

Denise's face softened and to her surprise, she found herself laughing. "I don't know why everybody made such a big deal about it. This is exactly what the kids at Chateau Remy wear for PE every day."

"Sometime you've got to tell me more about that place," Jennifer said. "It sounds like something out of a movie."

"It was wonderful," Denise said wistfully. "I can show you some pictures at the sleep-over. Do you think these will look okay?" she asked suddenly, holding up a pair of baggy blue shorts.

"Do you want the truth?" Jennifer kidded.

"That's what I was afraid of." Denise stood up and made a face. "I guess I'd better wear them anyway. I don't think I'm ever going to find a pair that's small enough."

"I'll throw this stuff back in the cupboard while you get changed," Jennifer told her. "I'll see you back in class, okay?"

Denise looked worried. "Oh, please, can't you wait for me? I'll only be a minute, honest. I just can't face going back in that gym alone." Without waiting for an answer, she stripped down to her underwear and started to wriggle into the faded blue shorts.

Jennifer tried not to stare at Denise's honey-colored silk underwear, but her expression gave her away. Denise's matching bra and pants were trimmed in frothy swirls of creamy lace. Jennifer had seen underwear like that in magazines, but would never consider buying anything like that for herself.

"What's wrong?" Denise asked casually, buttoning her blouse.

"Nothing, I — " Jennifer swallowed. How could she admit that no one she knew dressed like that? Unconsciously, she fingered the strap on her own white cotton bra. She was tempted to tell Denise not to let Susan Hillard see her in the fancy underwear, but couldn't think of a polite way to say it.

Denise tossed her silky blonde hair over her shoulder and studied herself in the grimy wall mirror. Her skin was glowing, and even the baggy uniform couldn't hide her tiny waist and long slender legs. Her cheeks were flushed with a rosy glow and her lips were accented with a touch of peach lip gloss.

"I can't believe it," Jennifer moaned. "You even look good in a *gym* outfit!"

"Are you kidding?" Denise said, her eyes meeting Jennifer's in the mirror. "I look awful. I look like a *lump!*"

"Some lump," Jennifer muttered. A shrill whistle from inside the gym made her jump. "Are you ready?"

Denise tucked her blouse in her gym shorts and rolled her eyes despairingly. "As ready as I'll ever be, I guess."

"Then let's move it," Jennifer urged. "I've got the feeling Mrs. Scott is all set to send out a search party!"

Chapter 7

"Are you going?" Lucy Armanson asked excitedly a couple of days later. She and Jennifer had ducked into the girls' room before class, and Jennifer was trying unsuccessfully to wind her long hair into a French braid.

"To Denise's party?" Jennifer mumbled through a mouth full of bobby pins. "Of course, I am. How about you?"

"I got my invitation yesterday," Lucy answered. Her dark eyes met Jennifer's in the mirror and she grinned. "With that fancy little calling card that has her name printed in violet ink. Class, right?" She lowered her voice and leaned close to Jennifer. "When I first saw the envelope, I thought I was being invited to the White House!"

"I know what you mean," Jennifer muttered. She stared at her and frowned.

When she'd read "Five Steps to a French Braid" in *Seventeen* the night before, it had all looked so simple. But in the harsh light of the girls' room, she knew it was a mistake. The heavy braid was hopelessly lopsided, and curly wisps of hair were already escaping around her ears. "Right over left, left over right," Jennifer muttered, twisting her thick dark hair into a coil. "You need eyes in the back of your head to do this," she said wryly.

"What are you trying to do?" Lucy said curiously. She fumbled in her bag for a peach lip gloss, found it, and held it up triumphantly.

"A French braid. Do you know how to do one?" Jennifer asked hopefully.

"Me?" Lucy shook her thick dark curls and grinned. "You know I'm strictly a wash-and-wear type." She peered at Jennifer's hair sympathetically. "What's wrong with the way you usually wear it — with barrettes, or in a ponytail?"

"Nothing, I guess. I've kind of outgrown those styles, though. I'd like something more. . . ." She paused, remembering the magazine article. ". . . sophisticated."

"Sophisticated!" Lucy hooted. "You've been hanging around with Denise too much," she said, shaking her finger at her playfully. "Look, Jennifer," Lucy said seriously, "I don't want to give you a big head, but you look great just the way you are."

"I don't know," Jennifer said doubtfully. She looked at herself in the mirror. She was wearing a tomato-red sweater with a pair of jeans that were faded to exactly the right shade of dusty blue. She looked okay, she supposed, but she was ready for a change.

"Well, whatever you do, make it quick," Lucy said practically. "Homeroom bell's going to ring in three minutes."

"Oh, darn it all," Jennifer said, yanking the pins out of her hair. "I'll have to try this another time."

"How about Friday night?" Lucy suggested, running a hand through her hair.

"What's Friday night?" Jennifer said absently.

Lucy rolled her eyes. "The big party at Denise's, silly!" When Jennifer looked blank, she rushed on, "Think about it," she said patiently. "If *anybody* knows how to do one of those fancy French hairstyles, it's got to be Denise."

Jennifer let her dark hair tumble around her shoulders and her face brightened. "That's right! Denise will know exactly what to do."

* * *

"Quiet, she'll hear you," Mia Stevens said warningly. She glanced at the cafeteria serving line where Denise was wavering between a tossed salad and potato soup.

"Hah! Are you kidding?" Susan Hillard's pinched face contorted in a smile. "You could land a 747 in here and no one would hear it." She pushed her tuna sandwich aside and looked around the table. "Okay," she said flatly, "who's going to the party and who's not?"

"Well, I'm certainly going," Mia spoke up. "Andy is going out of town with his parents that night and I don't want to sit home alone."

"Where is Andy, by the way?" Tracy asked curiously. "It seems funny to see just one of you."

"And just what do you mean by that?" Mia's blue eyes, rimmed with heavy charcoal liner, flashed angrily. She was wearing a pair of tight animal print pants with a pink and white checkered sweater vest. Heavy silver earrings dangled down to her shoulders, and her tawny hair was fluffed out in a spiky mane around her face. She looks just like the cowardly lion in *The Wizard of Oz*, Jennifer thought.

"Nothing," Tracy protested. "You're always together, that's all."

"Oh, Mia, don't be so touchy," Susan

said impatiently "Everyone knows the two of you are practically Siamese twins."

"We're very close," Mia admitted. "Do you know, sometimes I know what Andy's going to say before he even says it?"

"I know exactly what you mean," Jennifer started to say. "In fact, sometimes Nora and I — " She broke off suddenly when Nora's foot prodded her under the table.

"It's been that way ever since I met Andy in seventh grade," Mia said dreamily.

"But where is he now?" Nora persisted. She looked around the crowded lunchroom, as if she expected Andy to materialize in his tight black leather jeans and ragged T-shirt.

"He's in detention," Mia said briefly. "I thought we were talking about Denise," she said, eager to change the subject.

"We are," Susan said, leaning across the table. "What did you guys think of the invitation? It looked like the Magna Carta, right?" she chuckled. "That heavy parchment paper, and where did she ever find *violet* ink?"

"I thought it was very pretty," Jennifer said loyally. She couldn't believe that Susan was saying such nasty things about Denise. She *had* been a little taken aback when she found the small gray envelope in her mailbox — nobody at Cedar Groves bothered sending out *invitations* to sleepovers — but who was she to criticize? Maybe that's the way they did things in Switzerland.

"Well, I'm going," Tracy piped up. "I wouldn't miss this party for the world."

"I thought you weren't crazy about Denise," Susan reminded her.

"I'm not," she said in her little-girl voice. "But she's got a brother, remember? A *gorgeous* brother."

"Get serious, Tracy," Nora said sharply. "Do you really think Tony Hendrix is going to hang around his kid sister's *sleepover?*"

"Of course I don't think he's going to *hang around*," Tracy said indignantly. "But he'll certainly be passing through from time to time." She toyed with her salad, and said thoughtfully, "Anyway, I'm kind of curious to see how Denise lives, aren't you?"

"I'm not *panting* to know," Susan said coolly. "I mean, I don't think I'll die if I don't find out what color her bedspread is — "

"Hi, everybody!" Denise appeared suddenly behind Susan, balancing her tray in one hand, and a notebook in another. Her voice sounded overly bright, Jennifer thought, as if she wasn't quite sure of her welcome, and had decided to bluff it through. She looked very beautiful in a plum knit sweater and black pants that were gathered at the ankles. Tiny silver earrings glinted through her blonde hair and she wore half a dozen thin silver bracelets on her wrist. "Room for one more?" she asked. A shy smile flickered over her face.

"Sure," Jennifer said, glancing at Susan. "Pull up a chair."

There was silence for a moment and no one seemed to pick up the conversation.

"Hey, I hope I'm not interrupting anything," Denise said, sensing that something was wrong.

"No, of course not," Jen said too heartily. "We were just talking about — "

"About PE," Amy Williams said quickly.

"Here we go again," Susan said with a heavy sigh. "Amy, you're the only person I've ever met who actually *likes* PE."

"Sure, I do," Amy said good-naturedly. "When I get to college, I want to major in it — "

"I don't believe it," Tracy said with a groan. "Amy, *nobody* majors in PE."

"That's what you think," Amy said, undaunted. "How about Mrs. Scott?"

"How about you, Denise?" Jennifer said.

"Did you like PE in Switzerland?" She smiled encouragingly.

"It was very different," Denise said slowly. "We didn't do as many exercises as you do —"

"You should tell that to Mrs. Scott," Tracy said feelingly.

" — because we spent a lot of time doing other things."

"Like what?" Jennifer asked.

Denise shrugged. "Horseback-riding, fencing, skiing. . . ."

"You did all that?" Tracy said, impressed.

Denise nodded and sipped her Coke. "And we had an Olympic-sized pool with a bubble top that was open all year round."

"It sounds like something out of a dream," Tracy said softly.

"It was," Denise answered. She was going to say more, when a deep male voice interrupted her.

"Denise, did you take my math homework off the kitchen table?"

"Omigosh, it's him!" Mia Stevens hissed. "Look, it's her brother, Tony." She nudged Amy Williams so hard, she sloshed chocolate milk all over her tray.

"I'm not blind, you know," Amy snapped. "I *know* who it is." She ran her fingers quickly through her short curly hair and fervently wished she'd had time to put on some lip gloss.

Tony Hendrix, looking unbelievably handsome in a navy and white ski sweater, was leaning over Denise, obviously unaware of the effect he was having on the whole table. Even Lucy Armanson was having trouble concentrating on her double cheeseburger, and was staring at Tony in openmouthed amazement.

"Well, did you or didn't you?" Tony was saying impatiently. "Because if you didn't, I'm going to have to jump off a bridge." His piercing black eyes were worried and he was out of breath, as if he had been running.

"Jump off a bridge? Hey, don't do anything that drastic," Tracy said coyly. "Math's not worth it." She waited for him to say something, but he ignored her and turned his attention back to Denise. Just what I need — another Steve Crowley, Tracy thought, annoyed. Why do I always pick the ones who are impossible?

"Relax, Tony. You're in luck," Denise said, reaching for her notebook. "It got mixed up with some of my papers. Sorry about that," she added, handing him a folder.

"I should murder you for this," he said, tapping Denise playfully on the head with the folder. "I thought I was going to have to redo five pages of quadratic equations." He tucked the folder under his arm and turned to go. "Sorry to have interrupted you," he said, his dark eyes sweeping over the table.

"See you Friday," Tracy said playfully. He gave her a blank smile and hurried down the aisle. She looked questioningly at Denise.

"He doesn't know about the sleep-over," Denise explained. "I better tell him today, or he might invite a bunch of his friends over to watch videos."

"That would be fine with me," Amy Williams said with a giggle. "I just hope all his friends look like him!"

"They *couldn't* look like him," Mia Stevens murmured. "He has got to be the best-looking boy I've ever seen." She grinned at Denise. "You're not really going to kick him out of the house Friday night, are you? I was kind of hoping we could watch *Dallas* together."

"We?" Tracy interjected. "You mean, just the two of you?" She made a face and tapped her head. "You're nuts if you think I'm going to let him out of my sight for a single minute! You're not the only one who thinks he's fantastic!"

"Yeah, I'm afraid Tony's going to be in

for a rough time Friday night," Lucy said to Denise. "He's going to have girls falling all over him."

"Well, he probably won't even be there. I really don't know what his plans are," Denise said casually. She wondered if the girls were serious. Tony still attracted a lot of attention every time he wandered over to her part of the school. In the beginning, she had thought it was because he was new, but now she realized that it was something else. He was definitely — what was that slang expression? A hunk.

The talk drifted to schoolwork, but Denise let her mind wander, as she looked around the cafeteria. She still didn't fit in at Cedar Groves, she thought. She didn't get lost anymore, and she had finally figured out her computer cards — but she was still an outsider. She glanced at Nora and Jen, deep in conversation. They were her first real friends here. Would she make others? Everything depended on the Friday night sleep-over, she decided. She had to make sure that everyone had a good time.

No, she had to do more than that. She had to make sure that everything was *perfect.*

Chapter 8

Denise looked at the tiny pig stretched out in the dissecting pan in front of her and tried not to shudder. They had done dissection in biology class in Switzerland, but it was always frogs and earthworms. Little things. Nothing like this fat, slippery, pink-skinned creature that looked like it was ready to wake up and jump off the table! Denise stared hard at it to see if there was any sign of life. Wouldn't it be awful if it wasn't dead — but no, that was crazy. It reeked of formaldehyde. Nothing could smell that bad and *not* be dead.

"Isn't this exciting?" Nora's bubbly voice broke into her thoughts. "You know, we're really lucky. Some schools make you wait until ninth grade to dissect pigs. Just look at this muscle structure — it's much more developed than I thought it would be," she went on cheerfully. She poked a pink leg tentatively with her scalpel and Denise winced. One of the pig's front feet was hanging over the edge of the pan, as if its owner were poised to escape.

"Very exciting," Denise said weakly. "But I've got to warn you, I've never done anything like this before. I'm afraid I'm not going to be much help."

"Oh, you'll get the hang of it," Nora said cheerfully. "Jennifer wasn't too thrilled with dissection at first, either."

Jennifer wrinkled her nose. "I can still remember that squid we did last year," she said feelingly. "Yuck!"

"How can you say that? That was one of our best dissections," Nora said in a hurt voice. "You know, Denise, the gastrointestinal system on the squid is really fascinating. It's a shame you missed it."

"Please," Jennifer said, holding up her hand. "I couldn't eat fish for a month after cutting up that awful thing."

"But that's crazy," Nora said patiently. "A squid is very different from what you normally think of as a fish. For one thing, it doesn't have any dorsal tail fins — "

"I don't care. It looked like a fish to me," Jennifer said flatly.

"I know," Denise muttered.

"You two are hopeless," Nora said absently. She was bending over the tiny pig, deftly wielding a scalpel, making a neat incision down the breastbone. "The circulatory system is very complex," she said. "We'll have to trace the path of the major arteries and veins, after we dissect the heart. . . ."

Jennifer looked at Denise and rolled her eyes. "She doesn't even know we're here," she said. She lowered her voice. "Nora usually ends up doing most of the dissection, and I do the drawings that we have to hand in. But if you want to do some cutting — "

"No, no, that's fine with me," Denise gulped. The last thing she wanted to do was pick up a scalpel. "I'm just glad that I have you two for lab partners."

Jennifer smiled at her. "I'm glad, too. Lab isn't my favorite class, and it's more fun if you have your friends with you."

They moved a few feet away and stared out the window.

"Is everything okay?" Jennifer's voice cut in.

"Sure," Denise said hastily. "I was just thinking about something."

"You looked like you were going to cry," Jennifer said slowly. She stared at Denise. Her enormous blue eyes were moist.

Denise bit her lip. How could she make Jennifer understand that she missed

Chateau Remy more than she'd thought she would? That she *belonged* there?

"No, I'm fine," she said, forcing a smile. She nodded toward Nora. "Maybe we'd better get back to work."

"Whatever you say," Jennifer said reluctantly. "There's no hurry, though." She made a face. "We're going to be working on Porky for the next six weeks."

Nora glanced over at Jennifer and Denise and fought back a wave of irritation. Why was Denise always horning in on the two of them? Of course it wasn't *always* Denise's fault. Sometimes she was just following Jennifer's lead. When Mr. Morris asked who could use a third partner for lab, Jennifer's hand had shot up before anyone else's, and she had asked for Denise. When Denise was assigned to join them, Jennifer had grinned from ear to ear like she'd just won the sweepstakes. So Jennifer was partly to blame, Nora decided.

"Having fun?" Steve Crowley's brown hair fell over one eye as he leaned down to look at Nora's pig. "Not bad," he said. "We messed up the capillaries on ours."

"You have to take little tiny swipes with the scalpel," Nora said enthusiastically. "Then you can separate out the arteries and veins and really see the pattern. It's amazing, isn't it?" she said, glancing down at the pig. "All those little red lines connecting like highways. . . ."

Steve laughed self-consciously. "The problem is, ours don't connect anymore. Your capillaries may look like highways, but ours look like a giant traffic jam. Everything's going in different directions." He lowered his voice. "I sure wish I had you for a lab partner, Nora, instead of Tommy Ryder."

"You got Tommy Ryder? How'd you manage that?"

"Bad luck," Steve said in a disgusted tone. "I'll be lucky if I get a C out of this dissection."

"That's awful," Nora said feelingly. She stared at him and was struck by how good-looking he was. His face was tanned and he had quick, intelligent eyes that were a startling shade of blue.

A sudden burst of laughter made them look up. Jennifer and Denise were standing side by side, giggling over a private joke.

"Speaking of partners," Nora said with anger, "I seem to have lost mine." She pointed with her scalpel in the direction of the two girls. "I guess Jennifer's decided to let me do the capillary system by myself."

"It's really something the way Jennifer

has taken that new girl under her wing," Steve said admiringly. "I see the two of them together all the time."

"So I noticed," Nora said bluntly. "You never see one without the other anymore."

Steve missed the sarcasm completely. "Yeah, that Jen is really something," he said seriously. "She just can't stand the thought of someone being left out."

"Apparently not." Nora was seething inside. It was bad enough to have Jennifer making a fuss over Denise, but now she had to stand here and listen to Steve singing her praises! It just wasn't fair. She decided to block Denise and Jennifer out of her mind and get on with her lab work.

"I've got an idea," Nora said suddenly. "Why don't you bring your pig — "

"Hamlet," Steve interrupted.

"You named your pig Hamlet?"

Steve nodded. "Cute. Why don't you bring Hamlet over, and I'll see what I can do with him. Maybe I can save some of those capillaries after all."

"Would you do that?" Steve said gratefully. "Hey, that's terrific. Don't go away," he added, hurrying down the aisle.

When he returned a moment later with his dissecting pan, Nora was horrified. "What happened to your pig?"

"I told you Ryder's hopeless at dissec-

tion. Do you think Hamlet can be saved?"
he asked worriedly.

Nora peered at the pig. "I think he needs
major reconstruction," she said slowly.
She picked up some thready red veins lying
on one side of the pan. "We need to do a
transplant," she said firmly.

"Whatever you say, Doc," Steve said
cheerfully. He leaned down and patted the
pig on the shoulder. "Relax, Hamlet. You're
in good hands."

"Neat pig, huh?" Mitch Pauley said at
the end of class. Denise tried to ease her
way past him, but Mitch's sturdy frame
seemed to fill the narrow aisle.

"Excuse me," Denise said curtly. The
bell had already rung, and she was deter-
mined not to be late for Italian class. Mr.
Mario's face drifted in front of her, just
as if someone had rubbed a lamp. The man
loved to mark her tardy!

Suddenly Tommy Ryder appeared and
gave Mitch a playful shove. "Can't you see
she's in a hurry?" he said loudly. He gave
a low theatrical bow to Denise. "Don't let
us keep you," he said, squeezing himself
against the lab counter.

Denise looked at him suspiciously and
then swept past him. She had only gone
a couple of feet when she felt Tommy
Ryder come up behind her.

"Which way are you headed? I'll walk you," he said, flashing his dazzling smile.

"Italian," she said briefly. "And I'm late."

"So I'll run you," he said, laughing. When Denise failed to laugh, Tommy snapped his fingers and shook his head regretfully. "I knew I should have signed up for Italian. What's it like?"

Denise shrugged and didn't slacken her pace. If this pest wanted to talk to her, let him run to keep up!

"Is it a pretty tough course?" Tommy asked, a little breathlessly. He fought back a feeling of annoyance. He had never had a girl ignore him like this, and he didn't like the feeling.

"I said, is it a pretty tough course?"

Denise glanced at him coolly. "Italian is very easy," she said smoothly. "Especially if you speak other Romance languages."

"Romance languages?" Tommy guffawed. "I'm all for that." He looked very pleased with himself.

Denise gave him a disgusted look, and his smile faded. "Romance languages," she said coldly, "like French and Spanish."

"Oh." It wasn't a brilliant remark, but it was the best he could do. For some reason, he felt hopelessly tongue-tied around

Denise. He knew he was miles ahead of the competition — Denise obviously wasn't impressed by jocks like Mitch Pauley, but he knew he had a long way to go before he could ask her out.

They came to the end of the corridor, and Denise dashed up the stairs two at a time. Her blonde hair flew out behind her as she turned the corner.

Maybe he could ask her out for a Coke or something after school — it wouldn't be like a real date. She suddenly slowed down, looking at the room numbers, and he knew he had to say something fast.

"Hey, Denise, what are you doing after school today?" He was making a superhuman effort to sound casual, but he knew his voice was tight and strained.

Denise had stopped in front of a classroom and turned to stare curiously at him. "Why?" Her voice was flat, expressionless.

"Because I thought. . . ." He hesitated and swallowed hard. She certainly wasn't making this easy for him. "I thought maybe we could grab a Coke or a hamburger or something." The words tumbled out over each other. Now she'd say yes, and in just a few hours he'd be strolling into the Pizza Den with Denise at his side. Heads would turn, and everyone would think what a great-looking couple they made. Only something was wrong. Denise was just staring at him, speechless.

"So . . . what do you say?" he asked, his mouth suddenly dry.

When Denise spoke, her voice was so low, he had to strain to hear her. She looked at him, her eyes cool, and said softly, "You've got to be kidding."

She turned and darted into class just as Mitch Pauley clapped him on the shoulder and said in a booming voice, "Way to go, man! Way to go!"

"Some girls have all the luck," Tracy Douglas said enviously. "Did you see the way Tommy Ryder went racing after Denise?" She peeled off the black lab apron and tossed it on the counter.

"I sure did," Lucy Armanson replied, "and it's the first time I've ever seen him make an idiot out of himself over a girl. Over *any* girl."

"That's the whole problem," Mia Stevens groaned. "Denise isn't just *any* girl, she's. . . ." Mia paused, apparently at a loss for words.

"Spectacular," Joan Wesley said.

"Let's get out of this place," Tracy said. She wrinkled her nose. "I can smell formaldehyde on myself — yuck!"

A few minutes later, she and Nora and Jennifer were making their way down the crowded corridor to study hall.

"I guess what really burns me up about Tommy Ryder," Tracy said, "is the way he acts like Denise is the only girl in the world." She tucked her red T-shirt into her jeans and pouted. "I've been dropping hints that I'd like to go out with him, for six *months* now, and does he notice? No! He acts like I'm invisible."

Nora and Jennifer exchanged glances. Who'd *want* to go out with Tommy Ryder? Jennifer wondered.

"That's too bad," Jennifer said sympathetically. "Maybe he'll suddenly surprise you and ask you out."

"Do you really think so?" Tracy asked eagerly. "You know, I could try something different. I could start wearing my bangs over to one side the way Denise does. Or maybe I should get a trim. I could get some of these split ends cut off."

Nora looked annoyed. "Tracy, do you really think that's going to make any difference?"

"Well, *something's* got to work," Tracy said wearily. "Of course there's always Tony Hendrix," she added, giving a sly smile. "Now there's a guy I could really go for."

"Isn't he a little old for you?" Nora asked.

"Not really," Tracy said defensively. She gave her T-shirt another little tug. "I can look lots older than thirteen." She peered at Jennifer. "You know, you should start wearing eye makeup."

"I do wear eye makeup." Jennifer turned and stared at her with her wide hazel eyes. "Dark-brown mascara, see?" She blinked her eyes rapidly.

"But it's not enough," Tracy objected. "With your dark hair, you could get away with a lot more. You should be using charcoal liner and layers of black mascara."

"Do you think so?"

Tracy nodded seriously. "Absolutely. And a little violet shadow on the lids and frosty pearl right under the brow would be fantastic." She paused. "You could probably look fourteen. Maybe even fifteen," she added generously.

"I'll think about it," Jennifer promised. She didn't dare meet Nora's eyes — she knew she'd start giggling.

"See ya'll later," Tracy said. "I've got to stop at the library."

The moment she disappeared down the corridor, Nora and Jen turned to each other and burst out laughing.

"A little violet on the lids," Nora mimicked in a squeaky voice. "I don't believe that girl! And why would you want to look fourteen?"

Jennifer shook her head and wiped her eyes. "I guess so I could attract the fabulous Tony Hendrix." She hugged her books to her chest and said thoughtfully, "Have you ever noticed that Tracy's whole conversation revolves around boys?"

"Tracy's whole *life* revolves around boys," Nora said flatly. "If Tony shows up at Denise's party, she's going to pester him to death." They came to a fork in the corridor and Nora said, "Going to study hall?"

"You go ahead and I'll catch up with you," Jennifer said quickly. "I want to duck into the girls' room first."

Moments later, Jennifer stared at herself in the square mirror over the sink. She was glad that no one was in the drafty, white-tiled room. She always felt self-conscious looking at herself if there were other girls around. She picked up a lock of dark hair and let it fall back to her shoulders, then she leaned close to the mirror and studied her enormous eyes. She tried to imagine how her eyelids would look if they were tinted violet. And what had Tracy said — frosty pearl shadow under the brow? She touched a dark eyebrow tentatively. She had never even *tweezed* her eyebrows, and wondered if she should start.

Denise wore eye makeup, she was sure of it. But it was done so cleverly, and the colors blended together so perfectly that it always looked really natural. She looked wonderful, even in bright sunlight.

Jennifer stared hard at herself. What worked for Denise wouldn't necessarily work for her, she admitted grudgingly. Her face was a completely different shape for one thing. It was long and thin, while Denise's was heart-shaped, with strong cheekbones, and a finely chiseled little chin.

All the teen magazines said not to compare yourself with other girls, but how could you avoid it? Jennifer wondered. According to Tracy, she was hopelessly behind everyone else — and not just in the makeup department either. Tracy couldn't seem to believe that Jen just wasn't interested in *dating* boys yet.

But Nora was exactly the same way, she thought gratefully. Nora never used a bit of makeup except lip gloss, and the idea of Nora dating — well, she just couldn't imagine it. "At least there's two of us," she said softly to her image in the mirror. She splashed her face with cold water and headed for the door.

Chapter 9

"Did you pack your pink snuggly pajamas or your yellow furry ones?" Nora asked Jennifer on Friday night. It was six o'clock and they were due at Denise's in half an hour.

"Yellow furry," Jennifer said absently, taking a look around Nora's room. It was very neat, as usual, and Jennifer was pleased to see her birthday gift — a pink calico cat cushion — perched on the bed.

Nora was busily packing a small navy-blue overnight case that was lying on the floor. She was wearing her best jeans with a white turtleneck sweater, and her curly brown hair was fluffed out around her face. "Which should I bring — my red Dr. Denton's or my Miami Dolphins night-shirt?"

"The Dr. Denton's," Jennifer said

promptly. "You might get too cold in the nightshirt."

Nora held the red pajamas up to her and said a little sheepishly, "They're the ones with feet. Do you think I'll look silly?"

Jennifer laughed. "Of course not. I bet a lot of girls will be wearing stuff like that. You're not the only person in the world with cold feet, you know." She wandered over to the dresser and began brushing her long black hair. She was dressed in jeans and a pale blue turtleneck sweater that was almost identical to Nora's. They had bought them together at a two-for-one sale at Steven's last August, and often traded them back and forth. "I wonder what Denise will be wearing?" she asked, staring at herself in the mirror.

Nora shook her head. "I can't imagine."

She snapped the suitcase closed and looked around the room. "I hope I haven't forgotten anything," she said, her eyes running over a small notepad.

Jennifer laughed. "Nora, you're the only person I know who makes a *list* of what to pack for a sleep-over."

"Toothpaste, blouse, pajamas, underwear. . . ." Nora ignored her and checked off the items one by one. "Well, I think that's it," she said cheerfully. She picked up the suitcase and headed for the door. "Ready to go?"

"I am, but you're not," Jennifer said. She stared at Nora, her hazel eyes wide and amused.

Nora looked at her blankly. "You mean I've gotten something?"

"I'll say! That floor's going to be awfully cold tonight."

"My sleeping bag!" Nora slapped her forehead and threw open the closet doors. "I must be losing my mind," she said, dragging a heavy duffel bag to the center of the room. "I can't believe I did that," she said, hoisting the shoulder strap over her arm. "I never forget anything!"

Jennifer rolled her eyes and followed Nora to the door. "There's always a first time," she kidded. "Anyway, you know something? It's nice to know you're human!"

"Denise, if you polish those candlesticks any more, you're going to wear a hole in them." Mrs. Hendrix smiled fondly at Denise, who was frowning over a heavy silver candelabra and biting her lip in concentration. "I don't know why you bothered putting out the silver and china, honey. You know Primavera's always brings their own when they cater a dinner."

"I know, but I wanted to do something special," Denise said, straightening up. She tucked a stray wisp of blonde hair behind her ear and checked the table. Everything looked perfect. She had used her mother's best English bone china and had covered the rosewood table with a snowy linen tablecloth. The leaded crystal glasses sparkled, and yellow and white mums tumbled out of a blue ceramic vase.

"I hope everything turns out the way you want it," her mother said, reaching for her coat. "Are you sure you don't need me?" She glanced at her watch. "I told your father I'd meet him at the club at six, but if there's anything I can do. . . ."

"No, everything's fine," Denise said.

"I've already paid Primavera's," her mother reminded her. "And there's extra ice in the freezer — "

"Mom," Denise interrupted her. "I'll be fine! Go ahead to your dinner party."

"If you're sure. . . . We won't be late."

The house seemed suddenly quiet when her mother had left, and Denise wandered into the huge, sprawling den and flipped on the stereo. The house looked beautiful, she decided. No one would believe they had just moved in a few months ago. The den was her favorite room. It had a high cathedral ceiling, and the creamy ivory carpeting was a nice contrast to the stark wooden beams. Her mother collected modern art, and dozens of bright paintings — all shapes and sizes — hung on the bleached oak paneling. The sofa was an enormous white sectional that snaked its way around the room. It was covered with bright silk pillows, and Denise reached down and absently plumped one up.

My first sleep-over in Cedar Groves, she thought nervously. Tonight is really going to be the turning point. She ran over the guest list in her mind. Nora Ryan and Jennifer Mann. She smiled to herself. I know I can count on them. They already like me. At least, Jennifer does. Nora is a little harder to get to know, but she'll come around in time. . . .

She walked back to the kitchen and checked the gleaming counter tops. Potato chips and popcorn filled giant wooden bowls and there was a whole keg of salted peanuts. Plenty of snacks and sodas for later on, when they would be watching videos. Her mind drifted back to her other guests. There was that girl who tried to dress like a punker, Mia Stevens. She seemed friendly enough, and had even admired some of Denise's clothes. Then there was that blonde who loved to flirt, Tracy Douglas. She seemed okay, but Denise had the uneasy feeling that Tracy was always checking her out, that she looked at Denise as competition. As if I'd be interested in those idiotic boys in our class! Denise thought, shaking her head. Then there was Lucy Armanson, who palled around with Jennifer, and Joan Wesley, the class genius. And Amy Williams, who wanted to teach PE. . . .

Denise forced down a panicky feeling. She paced restlessly around the room, and was just about to plump another pillow when the door bell rang. The party was starting!

She smiled, took a deep breath, and went to the door.

"Will you listen to that!" Lucy Armanson said, laughing. "I never thought I'd hear door chimes that play 'Strawberry Fields Forever.' " She was standing on the wide front porch, admiring the imposing stone house. "Something tells me tonight is going to be full of surprises, Jen."

"I'm already surprised," Jennifer said seriously. She turned to look down the long winding drive. Dozens of tiny lanterns lined the flagstone walkway, and they cast a soft yellow glow over acres of velvety grass. "In fact, I'm in shock. This place looks like something out of *Dynasty*."

"Or *Lifestyles of the Rich and Famous*," Nora said, her voice heavy with sarcasm.

"Don't you like it?" Jennifer asked.

"I just mean it looks like something you'd see on a television show," Nora said, not bothering to hide her disapproval. "It's hard to believe someone actually *lives* here."

Jennifer looked at her, puzzled. She knew that Nora wasn't as impressed as she was, and she wondered why. Usually they agreed on *everything*. The house was amazing, she thought, staring at the shimmering waterfall at one end of the terrace. It spilled into a kidney-shaped pool ringed with tropical palms.

Lucy rang the chimes again. "Hey," Jennifer protested. "You already rang once. I'm sure someone heard us."

"I can't help it," Lucy said with a giggle. "I'll probably never get a chance to do anything like this again." She put her hands on her hips and sighed. "When I get rich and famous, I want a house just like this. Denise has got to be the luckiest girl in the world!"

"And doesn't she just know it!" Nora murmured.

The door opened then to reveal a smiling Denise.

"Hi, everybody!" Denise ushered them inside. "You're the first ones to get here. Just dump your stuff on the floor, and I'll show you where your rooms are later." She was wearing white leather pants with a black tunic top, and her high heels clattered across the blue-tiled floor.

"Is it okay to walk on this?" Lucy kidded. "It looks like something out of a museum."

"They're hand-painted Italian tiles," Denise said casually. "Not very practical, but my mother saw them and fell in love with them." She clasped her hands behind her back. "Do you want to go in the den and wait for the others? We're not eating till seven-thirty."

"Seven-thirty? I'm glad I ate a big lunch," Nora said bitingly. She couldn't take her eyes off the gigantic planter that dominated the entrance hall. It held masses of towering green plants — some looked like small trees — that poked their way up to the glass skylight.

Jennifer stopped in her tracks when she saw one that was covered with tiny orange balls. "Ooh, look at the oranges!" she said delightedly. "Are they real?"

"No, they're plastic," Nora muttered, and Jennifer frowned at her.

Denise paused and peered at the tree. "They're real. That's a Seville orange tree," she said, touching one of the delicate green leaves. "Mom had it imported from Spain. It's doing pretty well here — I guess because it gets a lot of light."

Jennifer turned to Nora, her eyes wide with excitement. "I've never seen anything like it, have you? Imagine — you could pick your own oranges for breakfast!"

"Imagine that," Nora said briefly. What's the big deal? she wondered. You don't have to grow oranges in your front hall — you can buy them right in the supermarket!

"I might take one home for a souvenir," Lucy Armanson said, and winked at Jennifer. She couldn't get over this place! She could hardly wait to get home and tell her brothers and sisters — no one would ever believe it. "Where is your mother?" she asked.

"Oh, she's having dinner at the club," Denise said with a little laugh. "I had to tell her over and over that I could manage by myself tonight."

"My mother's the same way when I have a sleep-over," Jennifer said. "She's always afraid that I'll burn the pizza or spill Coke all over the rug."

"Just pick out whatever music you like, and I'll get us something to drink," Denise said when they got to the den.

She disappeared into the kitchen and Lucy gave out a low whistle. "Wow — what do you guys think of this?" She sank down into the deep white sofa and closed her eyes. "I think I'll stay here forever," she murmured. "What kind of music does she have?" she asked Nora, who was busily inspecting a stereo system that covered an entire wall.

"Everything from the Beatles to Billy Idol," Nora said wryly. "She could open a record store — she's got hundreds of tapes and albums, and even some old forty-fives."

"Wow! It's like having a personal juke box," Lucy said, peering over her shoulder. "I wonder if it takes quarters," she kidded.

Nora stared at the control panel and shook her head. "I think you'd need a pilot's license to work this thing. I've never seen so many buttons and meters in my life."

"It's easy when you get the hang of it," Denise said suddenly. She had kicked off her high heels and had entered soundlessly on the thick pile carpet. "Tony's the electronics nut in the family, but I can do the basic stuff. What do you want to hear?"

"Do you have anything by the Stones?" Lucy asked.

"Old or new?"

"I like their old stuff better." Lucy had

opened her eyes and was perched on the edge of the sofa.

"Here you go," Denise said, pulling out an album. She flipped a switch and in a moment, the pounding sound of "Start Me Up" filled the room. She passed out Cokes and pretzels with a shy smile. "I'm not putting out too many snacks, because I don't want anybody to lose their appetite for dinner," she said. "We're having something really good."

"Pepperoni pizza?" Jennifer asked.

"No, but it's Italian," Denise promised. "You'll like it, believe me."

Lucy snuggled down into the sofa and sighed happily. "I already do."

A few minutes later, the doorbell rang again, and within minutes, the den was filled with the sound of giggling girls. "I don't *believe* this place!" Jennifer heard Tracy Douglas say. "I almost expected a *butler* to open the door!"

"He's off this weekend," Denise said, and no one knew whether she was joking or not.

After taking a quick look around the room, Susan Hillard settled herself on the sofa next to Lucy. "Pretty showy, isn't it?" she said with a sly smile.

"*Sho-w-y?*" Lucy asked slowly, dragging

the word out to three syllables.

Susan shrugged. "You know, showy. Flashy." She tapped the marble coffee table and made a face. "Look at this table — it's probably genuine Formica."

Lucy ran her hand over the cool Carerra marble and laughed. "You're wrong. Denise told us all about this table. They had the marble shipped here from some quarry in Italy."

"Well, you'd never know it to look at it," Susan said nastily. She was about to say something else, but Lucy turned her head and began talking to Amy Williams. She was darned if she was going to let Susan Hillard spoil one of the most exciting nights of her life!

"Isn't this great?" Amy asked, her round face flushed with excitement. "I feel just like a movie star."

"Me, too," Lucy said contentedly. "I think I could get used to this. Say, Denise," she called across the room. "How about if we all just move in — for good?"

"That's fine with me," Denise said. "I miss having a bunch of roommates, like at the Chateau."

"You do? Living in a dorm couldn't be anything like this," Jennifer said, looking at the sliding glass doors that led onto a flagstone patio. "You wouldn't have your own room, or have any privacy."

"No, we did," Denise explained. "There were two girls assigned to each suite — "

"You had a *suite*?" Lucy asked, her dark eyes wide with surprise.

Denise nodded. "A bedroom, sitting room, and bathroom." She was sitting on a throw pillow on the floor and she tucked her long legs under her. She laughed. "I used to pretend that I was a princess when I first went there."

"She thinks she's a princess here," Nora said under her breath. Lucy Armanson gave her a warning look, and Nora innocently reached for her Coke.

The doorbell rang and she scrambled to her feet. "Excuse me, I've got to see about dinner," she said, heading for the front door.

"She must have ordered pizzas after all," Lucy said. Everyone was quiet, listening to a buzz of conversation in the front hall.

"They certainly sent a lot of people to drop off a few pizzas," Amy said, puzzled. "It sounds like there's a whole crew out there."

"And you know what? It doesn't smell like pizza," Lucy said, getting up. A delicious aroma drifted in the den and Lucy smiled. "I'll say one thing about Denise — she sure knows how to throw a party!"

Chapter 10

"Come in!" Denise was grinning from ear to ear as she threw open the doors to the dining room. "Sit anywhere you want," she said, pulling out one of the delicate rosewood chairs.

"This is unbelievable," Jennifer said dazedly. She looked at Nora, who seemed to be in shock, and stepped into the room.

"It's like a palace," Nora said, her eyes skimming over the glittering chandelier and yellow satin drapes. Then she looked at the long table heaped with gleaming silver serving dishes.

"Where did you get all this?" Jennifer asked.

"The food? It's from Primavera's," Denise said breezily.

"So that's what all the commotion at the door was about — we thought you had ordered pizzas!" Lucy piped up. "But where did everybody go?" She looked at the door to the kitchen as if she expected someone to appear.

"Oh, the caterers just put out all the food and left," Denise said, sitting at the head of the table. "They'll come back tomorrow and clean up all the mess."

"It must be nice," Susan Hillard muttered. She was sitting at the opposite end of the table — as far away from Denise as possible — and wondering what to do with all the silverware in front of her. There seemed to be *two* of everything — forks, knives, spoons — and she couldn't for the life of her figure out why.

"I hope everybody likes Italian food," Denise said, filling one of the plates and passing it down the length of the table.

"This looks good, but it doesn't *look* Italian," Tracy said, handing the dish to Susan.

That's got to be the understatement of the year! Nora thought, peering at the steaming dishes. How can you have Italian food without any pizza or spaghetti?

"It's *Northern* Italian. Chicken in marsala, *gnocchi verdi*, and there's lots of marinated vegetables and salads," Denise said, lifting a heavy china tureen. "Why don't we let Nora be the guinea pig?" she added. "How's the food, Nora?"

Everyone watched as Nora took a bite of chicken. It was tender and delicious with a light sauce. "Very good," she admitted reluctantly. She was on the spot, and she knew it. She managed a weak smile. "In fact, it's terrific."

"Score one for Denise," Nora mumbled under her breath. She glanced down the table at her hostess, who was sitting very straight in her high-backed chair. Her blonde hair was swept off her forehead in a tortoiseshell clasp, and her blue eyes looked enormous in the soft candlelight. She looked very poised and self-assured, and Nora felt a flicker of annoyance. She's putting on her princess act again, she thought suddenly, and we're all supposed to play the part of loyal subjects!

"This is really great food, Denise," Jennifer said enthusiastically.

"Yeah, it's super," Tracy gushed. "Isn't it, you guys?" She looked around the table. "What's the green stuff in the gnocchi, Denise?"

"Spinach. That's why they call it *gnocchi verdi*. *Verdi* means green in Italian," she explained.

"Spinach?" Lucy wrinkled her nose. "Well, it looks great anyway," she said, digging into her dinner.

Everyone was silent for a moment, and

then Tracy said wistfully, "Your brother's missing a wonderful dinner. It's too bad he's not here to enjoy it."

"You mean it's too bad we can't enjoy him!" Mia Stevens said, and got a laugh.

"You know he's not your type, Mia," Lucy offered. "You're just lonely because Andy's away."

"Tony Hendrix is *anybody's* type," Mia answered between mouthfuls of salad. "He's gorgeous!" She grinned and looked at Denise. "Tell me something, Denise. Does he go in for punk clothes? Or should I go home and change?"

"You look wonderful the way you are," Denise said tactfully. Mia was wearing a pink brocade jacket over a pair of tight pink and yellow pants in a wild floral print. She had spiked her orangey hair out more than usual, and was wearing a gold earring in her left ear.

"This isn't anything like I expected," Nora said quietly to Jennifer after dinner. Everyone had piled into Denise's room to watch videos on an oversized screen, and Nora and Jennifer were perched at the foot of Denise's brass bed.

"I didn't realize people lived like this," Jennifer said, her eyes roaming over the pink, plum, and white bedroom. "It's beautiful, isn't it?" she asked softly.

Nora wrinkled her nose. "A little flowery, don't you think?" She ran her hand over the gay chintz bedspread. "All these daffodils make me feel like sneezing," she teased.

"Don't you dare. This is one of those *designer* bedspreads," Lucy Armanson whispered.

"That's nice," Jennifer mumbled, resting her head on the soft quilt. She yawned twice and looked around the room. It was nearly midnight, and she was used to going to bed earlier. She tried to focus on the television screen, but the images kept blurring together. She was just about to drift off to sleep when the door to Denise's room burst open.

"Hey, Denise, I can't find—" Tony Hendrix stopped dead in his tracks and peered at the girls sprawled around the room. "Sorry," he said, hastily backing out the door.

"What's your rush?" Tracy Douglas purred. "Don't forget, I saw him first," she said teasingly to Amy Williams.

Mia Stevens said, "Why don't you join us?"

Tony gave a weak smile and was about to make a quick getaway, when Denise intercepted him. "Tony, don't be such an idiot," she said, sliding off the bed. "Nobody's going to bite you. What do you want?" She pulled him back into the room, laughing. He was wearing a pale blue sweater with a pair of faded jeans.

"I was wondering what happened to that new video we bought — the Springsteen one," he said quickly.

"It's downstairs in the den," Denise said. She tightened the belt on her black silk tunic and curled up on the king-sized bed. "Of course, you can always stay and watch the late show with us," she said with a grin. "Is that okay with everybody?"

"It's more than okay," Amy Williams said enthusiastically. "You can even share my popcorn."

"Thanks, but I, uh, think I'll go downstairs," Tony said wryly. He smiled and his teeth looked very white against his olive skin. "See you at breakfast." He gave a little wave and disappeared.

As soon as the door closed after him, Tracy Douglas rolled backward on the bed, and said dramatically, "I could die right now and be happy."

"You're a nut!" Lucy said, pretending to smother her with a pillow. "He's much too old for you."

"Yeah, but he's so gorgeous!"

"I'll say!" Mia Stevens said with a giggle. "If I ever get fed up with Andy, I'll know who to call." She paused. "Is he going out with anybody?"

"Nobody special," Denise answered. "We used to double-date sometimes when we both lived in Geneva. I'll say one thing for Tony," she continued, "he's got good taste in friends." She reached over and slid open the top drawer of her white wicker night table. "This is one of the guys he introduced me to."

She pulled out a picture and handed it to Tracy. "That's Jean-Paul," she said casually. "He was my . . . I guess you'd call it a 'one-and-only' over here."

"You went steady with him?" Jennifer said, surprised. She leaned forward to get a better look at the boy in the picture. He looked about eighteen, with long dark hair that fell over one eye. "How old is he?"

"Sixteen," Denise said briefly.

"Sixteen?" Nora looked at Jennifer. She couldn't imagine going out with someone sixteen! It would be hard enough to figure out what to say to someone *thirteen!*

Nora tried to catch Jennifer's eye, but she was staring at Denise, spellbound. So were the rest of the girls, Nora noted disgustedly. No wonder Denise seemed different. She really *was* from another world!

* * *

"I thought I'd put you and Nora in the blue room," Denise said to Jennifer later that night. "Then Lucy and Amy can take the green room, and Susan and Tracy can take the study. Let's see, that leaves Mia and Joan . . . they should have the rose room, I think. It's got really neat wallpaper. My mother just redecorated it." Denise scrambled off her bed and motioned for everyone to follow her down the long carpeted hallway. "Okay, gang, let's go."

"Wait a minute," Tracy piped up. "You said that Susan and I are staying in the study? It sounds like something out of a Clue game!"

Denise laughed. "Oh, we just call it that because it has a fireplace and these gigantic bookcases," Denise explained. "Actually, it's the same as all the other bedrooms. It has two double beds, a bathroom, and a little balcony."

"Let me get this straight," Nora said, heaving her duffel bag over her shoulder with a little grunt. "Do you mean you've got enough bedrooms for *everybody?*"

"Of course," Denise said, surprised. "I'm putting you two to a room, so you can have company." She paused. "What do you usually do at sleep-overs?"

Tracy hooted. "We usually rough it and

sleep on the floor!" she said. She pointed to her red Snoopy sleeping bag. "That's why we came prepared."

"Oh," Denise said, looking perplexed. "I didn't realize, but if you'd rather. . . ."

"Sleep on the floor instead of a bed? No way," Tracy said firmly. "I'm not working toward a merit badge — just point me to the study!"

This is like a fairy tale, Jennifer thought a few minutes later. She and Nora were sharing a powder-blue and white bedroom in the west wing of the house, and had just finished putting on their pajamas.

"I can't believe we have our own room," Jen said happily. "Imagine having a house with six guest rooms," she added, peering out a French door. "Oh Nora, come look — there's the balcony Denise told us about!"

"Wonderful," Nora muttered, rummaging through her overnight case. "If we had boyfriends, we could play a scene from *Romeo and Juliet*." She ducked her head back in her suitcase, and counted slowly to ten. She knew if she heard one more word about Denise and her fantastic house she was going to scream!

"I could stay here forever," Jennifer said, waltzing around the room. She picked up a silver-backed brush from a mirrored vanity table and ran it through her long dark hair. "I'd swim in the pool and soak in the jacuzzi, and when I got bored with that, I'd watch every single one of those videos." She giggled. "And whenever I got hungry, I'd pick up the phone and call Primavera's. . . ."

"Sounds like heaven," Nora said sarcastically.

"It sure does," Jennifer answered wistfully. She paused and stared thoughtfully at her friend. "What in the world are you doing?"

"What does it look like I'm doing?" Nora retorted. She carefully peeled the sky-blue floral quilt off the bed and replaced it with her sleeping bag.

"You're going to use your beat-up old sleeping bag on the bed?" Jen said incredulously.

"I brought it, and I'm going to use it," Nora said flatly. She looked at the satiny quilt and sniffed. "That thing doesn't even look warm. I suppose it's just for show — like the rest of the house."

"Hey, Nora, what's bugging you anyway? You've been in a funny mood all night. And I noticed you hardly touched your dinner."

"Maybe I wasn't hungry," Nora snapped. And maybe I'm sick of hearing

Denise's name every two seconds, she added silently. She took a final look in her suitcase and straightened up. "I've got a more important problem anyway," she said. "You didn't bring an extra toothbrush, by any chance, did you?"

"No, but I bet Denise has one," Jennifer said, heading for the door. "Knowing Denise, she probably has one for every day of the week."

"In designer colors," Nora said under her breath.

Together, they padded down the hall to Denise's room, their slippers sinking into the deep yellow carpet. Jennifer knocked softly, and Denise opened the door immediately. She was wearing a pair of white satin pajamas, and her blonde hair hung loose around her shoulders.

She smiled, puzzled. "Are you guys hungry? I bet you're in the mood for a midnight snack," she said. "There's plenty of dessert left over in the kitchen —"

"No, we're stuffed," Jennifer told her. "Dinner was fantastic, wasn't it, Nora?"

"Fantastic," Nora said, putting as little enthusiasm into the word as possible.

"Nora forgot her toothbrush," Jennifer said, stepping into the room. "And I told her I just knew you'd have an extra one laying around."

"As a matter of fact, I do. I just have to remember where it is." She threw open the double doors to a walk-in closet. "I'm sure I can find one inside my suitcase." She grinned at Nora. "I try to leave new ones in every single suitcase, because that's the one thing I always forget."

Jennifer looked pleased. "You see, you and Denise have a lot in common," she said to Nora.

"I never forget anything," Nora said stiffly. Jennifer stared at her, and she blushed. "Well, hardly ever."

"This might take a few minutes," Denise said. "My closet is kind of a mess. My mother's been bugging me to clean it out, but somehow I never get around to it."

"If it's too much trouble, don't bother," Nora began. She wished she had never mentioned the darn toothbrush! Now they'd be stuck in a long conversation with Denise.

"Oh, it's no trouble. Let's just pull a few of these out, and look through the side pockets." She started to drag out a matched set of creamy tan luggage.

Nora ran her hand over the satiny leather, and she thought of her navy blue duffel bag, bursting at the seams. Leave it to Denise, she thought bitterly. Even her *luggage* is perfect!

"Denise," Jennifer said suddenly, 'I

can't believe this! You've got the most terrific clothes I've ever seen." She stepped deeper into the closet, and began thumbing through a rack of dresses. "You could practically open a boutique."

"Not quite," Denise said, searching through an overnight bag. "Some of the stuff is from last season. If you'd like to borrow anything, go right ahead." She peered at Jennifer. "We're probably the same size. Seven, right?"

Jennifer made a face. "Sometimes a nine in pants."

"Hey, you know what? I've got something that would look great on you." Denise scrambled to her feet and lifted out a shimmery pink silk minidress. "This was in *Seventeen* last month," she said casually. "Pink is really your color," she said, holding it up against Jennifer. "It would look much better on you than it does on me. Your dark hair really sets it off."

"I think I found the toothbrush," Nora said happily, digging deep into a zippered compartment. Hurray! she thought. Now we can get out of here.

Denise and Jennifer ignored her. "Do you really think this is right for me?" Jennifer was asking, staring at herself in the mirror. "I usually try to wear blues and greens."

"You should go with warmer colors. Definitely," Denise replied. "Look how great you look in pink. It really shows off your complexion." She stood behind Jennifer and stared at her thoughtfully. "Tell me something. Do you always wear your hair like that — down around your shoulders?"

"Yep, this is definitely a toothbrush," Nora said loudly. She held up the plastic-wrapped toothbrush triumphantly. They'd have to answer her now!

"Uh-huh," Jennifer said, without bothering to turn around. "It's funny you should mention that, Denise, because I've been dying to try a French braid."

"Jennifer," Nora began, "it's getting late."

"A French braid!" Denise said. "I'm an *expert* on them!"

"You are?" Jennifer's face was glowing.

"I sure am. My roommate taught me how to do them. It's really easy once you get the knack of it."

"Do you think you could show me how?" Jennifer said excitedly.

"Sit down," Denise said, pulling out a chair in front of her dressing table. "You've got the perfect hair for a French braid. It's just the right length and it's really thick."

"I hope you're right," Jennifer said,

sliding into the chair. "I'm all thumbs when it comes to my hair. I tried to follow the diagrams in a magazine, but it was hopeless."

"You can't learn how to do a French braid from pictures," Denise said flatly. "You need the expert touch."

"And you've got it," Nora said under her breath. She stood up, clutching the toothbrush. "I'm going to turn in, Jennifer, I'm really wiped out." She headed for the door.

"Oh, sure," Jennifer said cheerfully. "See you later."

"Glad you found the toothbrush," Denise offered.

"Yeah, great," Nora said softly. She paused with her hand on the doorknob and looked back at them. They were staring in the mirror, talking, laughing together like they had been friends for years. As far as they were concerned, she was already gone.

She stood there for another moment, and then quietly let herself out the door. She had a lump in her throat, and a funny, tight feeling in her chest. She knew exactly what it was.

She was jealous.

Chapter 11

Nora took a deep breath. She didn't want to risk hurting her best friend's feelings, but she simply *couldn't* let Jen walk around for another minute with that droopy French braid trailing down her back. It was Monday afternoon, and Jen hadn't touched her hair since Denise had braided it at the Friday night sleep-over. She sneaked another look at her friend. There was no doubt about it, Jen was starting to look *wilted!*

"Jen," Nora said cheerfully as they stashed their books in their lockers, "don't take this the wrong way, but, um, how long are you going to wear your hair that way?" She thought she was being very diplomatic, but to her surprise, Jennifer turned to her with a frown.

"What's *wrong* with my hair?" she asked coolly.

"Well, nothing," Nora answered, taken off guard. "It's just that it's coming unraveled a bit in the back. You probably can't see it without a mirror," she said generously. "And there's a few loose ends here in the front," she added, brushing some stray wisps of hair off Jen's forehead.

"It's *supposed* to look like that!" Jen snapped. "Honestly, Nora, if you bothered to read any fashion magazines, you'd know that these are called *tendrils*."

"Tendrils?" Nora tried to keep a straight face, but she was afraid she was going to burst out laughing. Since when was Jen interested in something called *tendrils?*

"Yes, tendrils," Jen repeated in an annoyed voice. "Denise left them out of the braid *deliberately*." She quickly checked her hair in a small mirror taped to the inside of her locker door. "It gives a softer look to my face."

"Oh."

Jen gave her hair a final pat and closed the locker door. "I know it needs to be done again," she admitted. "Denise warned me it would only last for a day or two, but I was afraid to take it apart." She smiled. "She's going to redo it for me this afternoon."

Denise, Denise, Nora thought, her heart

sinking. Jennifer had talked of nothing else since the sleep-over.

"Right after we go shopping."

Nora was spinning the dial on her combination lock, when her hand froze. "What did you say?"

"We're going shopping at the mall," Jennifer repeated, as if it was the most natural thing in the world. "Do you remember I saved some of my birthday money?" she chattered on happily. "Well, Denise is going to help me put together a whole new wardrobe. A whole new *look*."

"That should be interesting," Nora said scathingly. "Especially on fifteen dollars." She knew the contents of Jennifer's piggy bank as well as her own.

"Fifteen dollars and seventy-six cents," Jennifer corrected her. "Anyway, Denise says it's not the *amount* of money you spend on your clothes that counts. It's how you put them together."

"I'll have to remember that the next time I go shopping," Nora muttered.

"All set to hit the stores?" Denise asked. She was wearing a plum-colored sweater, over a long paisley skirt that fell well below her knees. Nora was sure she had the sweater on backwards, because the deep V neckline plummeted down her back.

Is that the way they're wearing them this year? she wondered. Denise's long blonde hair was pulled into a sleek French braid and she wore thin gold hoop earrings.

"Denise, you look beautiful!" Jennifer said with admiration. She turned to Nora with a dazzling smile. "Doesn't she look just gorgeous?"

"Gorgeous," Nora said and picked up her books. "Look, if you two have plans, I don't want to keep you." She was making an effort to sound casual, but deep down she was stung. Jennifer *never* went shopping without her!

"Don't you want to come with us?" Denise asked. "We'll get Jennifer all fixed up, and then we'll go back to my place."

"Of course she's coming with us!" Jennifer said, linking her arm through Nora's. "We always do all our shopping together," she explained to Denise. "Isn't that right, Nora?"

Nora felt a wave of relief wash over her. "That's right," she agreed. So far, she added silently.

"I always stop at the perfume counter first," Denise explained later that afternoon. She picked up a graceful swan-shaped bottle from the counter at Bradley's and sighed. "You just don't have the range of perfumes here that you have in France."

"No?" Jennifer asked. "I mean, no, that's certainly true," she said hastily. She looked at the array of brightly colored bottles and wondered why anyone would *want* to have more choices.

Denise unstopped the plunger on a cut-glass bottle and waved it gently in the air. She sniffed delicately and made a face. "Too heavy," she pronounced and replaced it on the counter. "You know, in the south of France, there's this little town called Grasse — "

"I know about Grasse," Jennifer said eagerly. "We studied it in French class."

"Well, in France, they can blend a perfume for you while you wait." She paused to let this sink in. "You can choose any flower you want — I like gardenia — and they crush the petals right in front of you."

"That's amazing," Jennifer said in awe-struck tones. "Did you hear that, Nora?"

"I heard," Nora said, irritated.

"Oh, I'm absolutely awful at choosing perfume," Denise said. "I have to sample everything in sight and it takes me *ages*!"

Jennifer shook her head sympathetically. "I know what you mean," she said feelingly. "I'm exactly the same way myself."

Nora stared at her. As far as she knew, Jennifer had worn perfume only once in her life. Her great aunt had given her a bottle of Lily of the Valley for Christmas, and she had doused herself with it, before breaking out in a bright red rash.

"Try this, Jennifer," Denise said, handing her a tester bottle of wild musk. "You just dab a little behind your ears."

"Jennifer," Nora began, "remember what happened last Christmas — "

"Oh hush, Nora," Jennifer snapped. "That was ages ago." She touched the stopper to her neck and leaned close to Nora. "What do you think?" she said seriously. "Is it right for me?"

Nora drew back, her nose stinging. "Yuck! What's in that stuff?"

"It's wild musk," Denise said lightly. "It's supposed to have an interesting animal smell."

Nora ran her hand over her nose trying to erase the lingering odor. "It reminds me of Sinbad," she said thoughtfully. "Before he has a bath."

"Sinbad?" Denise arched her perfectly shaped eyebrows.

"Her pet hamster," Jennifer said in icy tones.

"Is something wrong?" Denise said pleasantly, noticing Jennifer's red nose and watery eyes.

"I'm fine," Jen said in a strangled voice.

"I guess I never realized that I'm allergic to all this stuff."

"Oh, gosh, I'm sorry," Denise said. "You should have told me." She scooped up a lemon-yellow-and-white striped box and handed it to the cashier. "We can be out of here in a minute."

Jennifer looked at the price on the box and gasped. "Denise, are you sure this is what you want?"

"I always try everything in sight, and then end up buying this," she said with a laugh. "Silly, isn't it?"

"Silly," Nora muttered. The small spray bottle was forty dollars. Twenty hours of baby-sitting! she realized with a shock. But then, she reminded herself, Denise probably has never baby-sat in her life!

"Well, are you happy with your new look?" Denise asked Jennifer a couple of hours later. It was nearly five o'clock, and she and Nora were sitting cross-legged on Denise's bed, as Jennifer posed in front of the mirror.

"I love it," Jennifer said, twisting around so she could see the back of her bright orange sweater. She was wearing the deep V in the back, just like Denise had done. Her dark hair was swept back in a French braid, and her hazel eyes glowed.

"I'm so lucky they had these on sale," she said happily. "I think it makes me look *entirely* different, don't you, Nora?"

"It's very nice," Nora said, staring into her cup of tea, thinking, I wish it was a Coke.

"It's more than nice," Denise said, scrambling off the bed. "She looks fantastic." She adjusted a loose hair comb, and looked at Jennifer's reflection in the mirror. "It's too bad there's not something special coming up. It would be fun to show you off. Don't you ever have any dances at Cedar Groves?"

Nora and Jennifer exchanged a look.

"Well, there's the Halloween Dance," Jennifer began. "But I don't think it's exactly what you had in mind. . . ."

"Why not?" Denise said gaily. "If there's boys and girls and music, it's a dance."

"Well, that's just it," Nora broke in. "There's girls and boys, but it's not a date-type thing. We go separately."

"Separately?" Denise stared at her as if she were crazy.

"We go in groups, I mean. Probably Lucy and Jennifer and I will go together this year," she explained.

"You're kidding!" Denise said in that same amazed tone. "I thought I'd seen everything in Europe, but you sure have

130

some funny customs here in Cedar Groves!"

The following week, Nora was saving a space at their usual table in the cafeteria when Jennifer came bounding up. "I hope you saved two seats," she said, plunking her tray on the table.

"Two seats?" Nora asked.

Jennifer nodded over her shoulder. "Denise is right behind me."

"Oh, great," Nora said, rolling her eyes.

"What's wrong?" Jennifer asked. "Don't you like her?"

"It's not that, it's just — "

She never got a chance to finish her sentence because Denise slid into an empty seat next to her. "Hi," she said cheerfully. "Did Jennifer tell you the good news?"

"I was waiting for you to get here," Jennifer said excitedly. "Guess what, Nora? They just posted the notice about the Halloween Dance, and you're looking at the new members of the theme committee!" She paused expectantly.

"You and Denise?" Nora asked.

"And you, too, silly." She unwrapped her tuna sandwich and took a giant bite. "We signed your name for you. We knew you'd want to do it."

Jen turned to Denise. "The Halloween Dance is the biggest event of the year here.

I'm so glad you're going to be part of it."

"Me, too," Denise said, spearing a wedge of tomato. She raised her Coke glass in a toast. "The three of us will make sure it's done right," she promised.

"But we've always had balloons and crepe paper streamers," Mia Stevens said heatedly. "I think they're cute." It was the following Monday and the theme committee was meeting in an empty classroom on the first floor.

"That's just the problem, Mia," Denise said patiently. "We're not looking for *cute* this year, we're looking for exciting . . . different . . . fantastic." She waited for Mia to say something, and then looked helplessly at Jennifer. "You understand what I'm getting at, don't you?"

"I think so," Jennifer said slowly. "You don't want to use the crepe paper witches and orange streamers we had last year."

Denise looked at the decorations spread out on the long table in front of them and shuddered. "I certainly don't. They're awful! Really tacky."

"Instead you want to have a costume ball and black-and-white decorations."

"That's right," Denise said, beaming. "I went to one just like it in London last year. It was fabulous! We had giant black-

and-white playing cards on the walls, and we strung black-and-white dominoes from the ceiling. . . ."

"I don't get it, do you?" Tracy Douglas whispered to Nora. "No witches or black cats?"

Nora smiled sympathetically. "I guess not," she said in a low voice. "But it looks like this is Denise's show," she added wryly.

"Yeah? Well, it's still our school," Tracy whispered hoarsely. "We should have *something* to say about the biggest dance of the year." She cleared her throat noisily. "Denise, I hope you realize we've only got a few dollars to buy new decorations." She pointed to a coffee can on the table. "That is the entire budget for the theme committee." She looked at the rest of the girls, sure she had scored a victory.

"Oh, money is no problem," Denise said breezily.

"Maybe not for you," Mia Stevens piped up.

"For any of us," Denise retorted. She clasped her long fingers together in front of her. "You may not realize this," she said calmly, "but my mother is on every single charity board in town."

"So?" Mia questioned.

Denise shrugged and leaned back in her

chair. "So, they have tons of dances with fabulous decorations and we can *borrow* whatever we need from them." She waited a moment. "No one has any objections to that, do they?"

"I guess not," Tracy said uncertainly. "It's just that we've never done it that way."

"Then this is the right time to start," Denise said, suddenly sitting up straight. "Now the first thing we need is the dominoes, and I happen to know that the Heart Foundation used some in a Mardi Gras ball last February."

"Wow! She really got everybody fired up," Tracy said admiringly at five-thirty that afternoon. The meeting had just broken up and she and Nora and Jen were walking home together.

"She certainly won *you* over," Nora pointed out acidly. "What happened to the it's-our-school-too bit?"

Tracy shot Nora a surprised look. "Well, I had second thoughts after she explained what she had in mind, didn't you? Everything Denise said made sense," she said.

"Like when she said, 'Why rough it when you can go first class?'" Nora kept her voice perfectly even, but she knew that Jennifer was staring at her.

"What's wrong with that?" Tracy challenged.

"Nothing, I guess." Nora sighed with resignation. "I just think that Denise is a little far-out for Cedar Groves."

"Well, I think she has a lot of imagination," Jennifer offered. "And if she can put together some first-class decorations for us, and not spend any money — "

"Then who are we to argue?" Nora finished for her.

They stopped at a red light and Tracy began a long monologue about a great-looking boy she had spotted in the public library. Jennifer listened politely, but Nora stared blankly into space, lost in her own thoughts. Denise is taking over everything, she thought to herself. The theme committee, the decorations. . . . She looked at Jennifer. Her newly braided hair shimmered in the late afternoon sunlight, and under her new orange sweater she wore a long paisley skirt. And worst of all, Nora thought, I think she's taking over my best friend.

Chapter 12

The next two weeks passed quickly, and Nora was so busy working on a science project that she almost forgot about the Halloween Dance. She was sitting up in bed studying one night, when the phone jangled.

"Nora?" Denise's low, musical voice leaped at her over the wire. "I'm in a mad rush, but I just want to remind you about the theme committee meeting tomorrow afternoon."

"Tomorrow?" Nora frowned. "I thought it was supposed to be next week — the twenty-third."

Denise laughed. "You must be working too hard. This *is* next week. Today's the twenty-second."

"Sorry about that," Nora muttered, rubbing her eyes. "I've been living and breathing biology," she apologized. "You see, I'm doing this really neat project on blood circulation — "

"I'm sure it's fascinating," Denise said hurriedly, "but I've got six more phone calls to make tonight. Maybe you could tell me all about it tomorrow," she added smoothly. "You *will* be there, won't you?"

Something about Denise's voice made it sound like a royal command, and Nora bristled. "Of course I'll be there," she said coolly. "When I say I'm going to do something, I do it."

"Great," Denise went on, ignoring Nora's icy tone, "because I've got a surprise for everybody. And a fantastic suggestion I want everyone to vote on."

Another fantastic suggestion? Denise never worried about false modesty, Nora thought. "I can hardly wait," she said, and this time the sarcasm in her voice was unmistakable.

"Terrific," Denise said, a little uncertainly. "See you then," she added, and hung up quickly.

Nora went back to her biology book, but she was sleepy, and the words began to blur on the page. What did Denise have up her sleeve? she wondered. She thought of calling Jennifer and stopped. She won't know any more about it than I do — I'll just have to wait till tomorrow.

* * *

"I thought it would be more fun to have our meeting here at Temptations," Denise said the following afternoon. The ice-cream shop was jammed with the after-school crowd, but Denise and her group managed to find an empty booth against the back wall. "Don't get me wrong," Denise said, sipping a frosted lemonade that was exactly the same shade as her scoop-necked sweater, "I like Cedar Groves Junior High, but after a whole day there, I'm ready to escape."

"Me, too," Tracy Douglas said feelingly. She started to dig into her hot fudge sundae and stopped, her spoon poised in midair. "Plus this is a great place to meet cute guys." She gestured to the front of the shop and gave a sly wink. "Check out the center aisle."

Nora looked up in time to see Steve Crowley settling down with a bunch of his friends. "It's just Steve Crowley," she blurted out in surprise."

"*Just* Steve Crowley!" Tracy repeated in a high-pitched voice. "Well, maybe that's all you see when *you* look at him, but I see one great-looking boy. Look at those broad shoulders . . . those eyes . . . the way his hair falls on his forehead. . . . He's adorable!"

"I second the motion," Mia Stevens chimed in.

"I third it!" Lucy Armanson said breathlessly, sliding into a tiny space next to Jennifer. "Sorry I'm late, but I had to help Mrs. Cooper clean up the science lab." She shrugged out of her red vinyl jacket and fluffed out her short dark hair. "Now, tell me, what did I just agree to?"

"I think you just agreed that Steve Crowley is adorable," Denise said, a little impatiently. She cleared her throat and tapped on her lemonade glass with a pencil. "Okay, if everybody's settled, let's get started."

"I'm not settled," Lucy objected. "I didn't even order anything yet."

Denise looked annoyed. "Really, Lucy," she began.

"Hey, no problem. You can share with us," Jennifer said quickly. She handed Lucy an iced-tea spoon and pushed a heavy glass dish toward her. "Nora and I are splitting a Kansas City Cyclone."

"My favorite," Lucy said happily. She scooped up a giant spoonful of whipped cream and smiled at Denise. "Don't let me interrupt you," she said with a twinkle in her eye.

"I'll try not to," Denise muttered. She waited until she had everyone's attention, then looked at a yellow legal pad. "I've got some great news," she said in her low voice. "My mom got in touch with the Heart Fund and they're letting us use all their decorations."

"Fantastic!" Jennifer said enthusiastically.

"And — wait till you hear the rest. My father is donating the refreshments."

"You're kidding!" Amy Williams looked at her in astonishment. "Do you have any idea how much that's going to cost?" Lucy Armanson kicked her under the table and she blushed. "Of course, if he really wants to do it . . ." she finished with an embarrassed grin.

"He really wants to do it," Denise said smoothly. "We've already called Primavera's and they're doing the works — meatballs, fondue, pizza squares, a vegetable tray, plus chips and dip."

There was a long pause, and then Amy Williams said admiringly, "You've thought of everything, Denise. You really have."

"You've done a great job," Tracy said, her blue eyes wide and serious. "Really super."

"Right on!" Lucy said, and touched her index finger to her thumb in an okay sign. "This is going to be the biggest thing to ever hit Cedar Groves!" There was an excited buzz of conversation then, and Nora automatically smiled and tried to look interested. She's really won them over, Nora thought. They don't seem to mind that she's taken over the group completely.

Denise waited for the conversation to die down and allowed herself a little smile. "I'm glad that everybody's happy with this . . . but there's something even more important that we've got to talk about."

This is what she was hinting at on the phone, Nora thought. She knew instinctively that all the talk about the decorations and food was just a warm-up to what Denise really had on her mind.

"I've got this fantastic idea," Denise began in her soft voice. "It came to me the other night when I was making all the plans for the decorations."

"She means when her mother was making all the plans," Nora muttered to Jennifer. "All she had to do was ask." Jennifer silenced her with a look, and Nora gave up and cupped her chin in her hand. She's probably going to fly Bruce Springsteen in for the night, she thought. With Denise, anything is possible!

"Hurry up and tell us," Tracy said. "I can't stand the suspense.

"Okay, here goes." And then Denise dropped the bombshell. "I think we should make this a Sadie Hawkins Day dance."

"What?" Jennifer looked at her blankly. "What is a Sadie Hawkins?"

"That's a character from *L'il Abner*," Lucy told her. "Once a year, in Dogpatch, the girls would chase the boys and ask them to marry them. And I think what Denise means . . . is that we should ask boys to the Halloween Dance, right?"

"Exactly." Denise looked pleased. "Everybody has to ask a date."

A date? Nora was stunned. "What if we don't know anyone?" she said, finding her voice at last.

"Nora, don't be silly," Denise said, tossing her blonde hair over her shoulders. She was wearing half a dozen silver bracelets and they clanked together when she raised her hand. "There are dozens of boys at Cedar Groves you could ask. Maybe *hundreds*." She paused. "After all, I've only been here a few weeks, and if I can come up with someone to ask, you certainly can!"

"But I don't understand — why are we changing things?" Jennifer asked. "After all, we went in a group last year — just girls — and everyone had a great time."

"That was different," Denise said patiently. "Last year you had balloons and crepe paper streamers, remember? This year it's going to be a real dance, Jen."

"The food sure sounds better," Lucy offered. "Last year, we had stale potato chips and warm Coke."

"Well, this year everything is going to be first class," Denise insisted. "It's going to be a night to remember. Now, doesn't it make sense to bring a date?"

The girls argued about it for an hour. Their voices grew louder and each of them gave her point of view. Finally, Denise said firmly, "Let's take a vote."

"I still can't believe it." It was the following Monday afternoon, and Jen was curled up on the window seat in her room, watching Jeff and Eric rake leaves. She was wearing a black sweater and a red plaid skirt and her long hair was hanging loose over her shoulders. "I can't believe we actually voted to bring dates!"

"Believe it," Nora said. She was sprawled on Jennifer's bed, thumbing through a class yearbook. "Anyway, we were forced into voting for it, don't you think? Once Denise and Tracy voted yes, the rest of us just went along. We didn't want to look like babies," she added glumly.

"Go through the list of possibles again," Jennifer urged.

"If you insist." She flipped to the front of the yearbook and gave a grim laugh. "We've been through the book three times, and I have to tell you, Jen, it doesn't get any better."

"Oh honestly, Nora, you're such a pessimist!" Jennifer jumped off the window seat and took the book away from Nora. "I bet there's just dozens of boys we haven't even thought of."

"Whatever you say." Nora tucked her hands behind her head and closed her eyes. "I'm open for suggestions."

"Okay," Jennifer said, settling down beside her. "Now, we'll just approach this calmly and logically. After all, it's not like we're going to spend the rest of our *lives* with these boys. All we need is a date for a dance."

"I'm all ears," Nora said. "So far, I haven't heard any names."

"I'm getting to it," Jennifer insisted. "Now should we do it alphabetically?"

"Spare me," Nora pleaded. "Let's go through all the boys we know first. We can start with the ones in our classes."

"That makes sense," Jen said calmly. "Let's alternate, okay? You say a name and I'll say a name. And no matter how crazy it sounds, we'll both consider it very seriously, okay?"

Nora nodded. "Scout's honor."

After ten minutes, both girls were convulsed with giggles. "Mitch Pauley," Jennifer said.

Nora howled. "Mitch Pauley — you've got to be kidding! I think I lose a few IQ points every time I talk to him."

Jennifer shook her finger reprovingly. "That's not very nice, Nora," she said, trying not to laugh. "Let's hear you come up with something better."

"Andy Warwick."

It was Jennifer's turn to howl. "Andy Warwick — he'd probably wear his black spiked dog collar!"

"Well, I happen to think he looks very handsome in it," Nora teased. "How about Tommy Ryder?"

"Impossible. He'd hide in the boys' room and stare at himself in the mirror all night. He's the most conceited boy I ever met!" She paused. "And you took two turns."

Nora flipped rapidly through the pages and said in a despairing voice, "Oh no — we're getting to the bottom."

"I think we've already *hit* the bottom," Jennifer said tartly. "What about Chuck Abernathy?" She pointed to a long-haired boy staring sullenly into the camera. "I haven't seen him around in ages."

"He spends his life in detention. And if

you're seriously considering Chuck Abernathy, we really *have* hit bottom." She closed the book and sighed. "What are we going to do?"

Jennifer hesitated. "I guess we could always tell Denise that we can't think of anybody."

"No, there's got to be a better way." Nora sat cross-legged on Jennifer's bed, twisting a lock of curly brown hair around her finger. The room was very still, and from outside, she could hear muffled shouts of laughter. She decided to take another look at the yearbook. All the boys they knew were hopeless, impossible. But Cedar Groves was a big school — surely there were two boys somewhere for them! The trouble was, how to find them? Suddenly her hand froze on the page. "That's it!" she said, jabbing her finger on a picture. She released her curl and it sprang back into a tight coil next to her head.

"You found dates for us?" Jennifer looked up, startled.

"No, but I thought of somebody who can help us," Nora said, snapping the book shut. "Get your jacket," she said, buttoning up her bright green windbreaker. "We're going to visit a friend."

Steve Crowley's brown hair was standing up in spikes and his navy running suit was rumpled when they saw him a few minutes later.

"Perfect timing," he said, taking a big gulp of water. "I just came back from a five-mile run." He stretched his long legs out in front of him, and the porch swing creaked dangerously.

"We need your advice," Nora began. She quickly explained about the Sadie Hawkins Day Dance and passed him the class yearbook. "We've put a check next to all the boys we *don't* want," she told him.

He flipped through the pages and whistled softly. "And you want me to come up with two perfect dates. You don't want advice, you want a miracle," he joked.

He started to pass the book back, but Jennifer stopped him. "Please, Steve," she said. "I know you can think of a couple of people. We're really desperate."

"Why do I let myself in for these things?" he muttered. "Okay, I'll take another look." He turned to the first page and ran his finger quickly over the page. "Nothing here," he murmured. "Or here," he added, turning to the next page. "Wait a minute — Charlie Bernard's in my Spanish class. He's a pretty nice guy. And Jim Blake is okay, too. He's on the soccer team — good sense of humor."

"Charlie Bernard, Jim Blake," Nora repeated, making notes on a legal pad.

"And Tony Clark and Matt Cobson are nice guys, too," Steve said, turning some pages. "They're both computer nuts."

"Hey, this is really great," Jennifer said happily. "Four names and we're not even out of the 'C's' yet. We're going to have dozens of boys to choose from."

"Don't get carried away," Nora reminded her. "We don't really know anything about them."

"We know that Steve says they're okay," Jennifer said loyally. "His word is good enough for me."

"But that doesn't mean they're going to be thrilled to go to a dance with us, Jen." Nora paused. "And just think how scary it's going to be, calling up a boy and asking him out. We've never done anything like this in our whole lives!"

Jennifer's smile faded. "You're right," she admitted. "It's going to be awful. Terrifying."

Steve laughed. "Now you know what boys have to go through."

Chapter 13

"Well, do you have somebody in mind?" Jennifer asked Nora when they left Steve half an hour later. It was nearly six, and the pale afternoon sun had vanished, leaving the air surprisingly chilly.

"Maybe yes, maybe no," Nora said mysteriously. She shivered and turned up the collar on her nylon windbreaker.

"What kind of an answer is that?" Jennifer challenged. "Either you found a date or you didn't."

"Let's say I think I know who I'm going to ask. Of course I've got no way of knowing if he'll say yes. He's pretty popular with the girls."

Jennifer thought for a minute. "Not Tommy Ryder!" she said after a minute.

Nora gave her a withering look. "Please — give me a little credit!"

"One of Steve's friends then — maybe

Charlie Bernard or Tony Clark?"

"I'd rather not say."

"What!" Jennifer stopped dead in her tracks and tugged at Nora's arm. "Since when are we keeping secrets from each other?"

Nora flushed. "I'm not keeping secrets," she insisted. "I'm just . . . look, won't it be more fun if we each pick someone, and let it be a surprise?" She ducked her head, and Jennifer couldn't tell if she was avoiding her eyes, or the biting October wind.

"Fun?" Jennifer said slowly. She couldn't understand why Nora was acting like this! "But we've always told each other *everything* before."

"I know," Nora said, in a more conciliatory tone, "but think how surprised we'll be when we finally see each other's dates at the dance."

Jennifer stared at her. "You really mean it — this is the way you want to do it?"

"Sure I do." She smiled warmly at Jennifer. "It will make things a lot more interesting. I bet you've got a name up your sleeve right now, don't you?"

"Well . . ." Jennifer began. She thought of the faces in the yearbook. She couldn't imagine spending five minutes with any of them, much less a whole evening! But she didn't want to be a spoilsport, so she said casually, "Well, there *is* somebody. . . ."

"I knew it!" Nora said triumphantly.
"Look, we'll make a pact," she said, as they
parted at a street corner. "We'll tell each
other the minute we get up the nerve to ask
someone, but we won't tell his name."

"Okay," Jennifer said. She wished she
could feel as lighthearted as Nora, but her
spirits were hovering somewhere down
around her ankles. She had the sinking
feeling that the Halloween Dance was going to be a disaster — at least for her.

"Cheer up!" Nora said, catching her
friend's long face. "This is going to be a
blast — you'll see!"

Nora waited until Jennifer turned the
corner and then quickly retraced her steps
to Steve's house. Her heart was beating
like a tom-tom in her chest, and she felt
curiously light-headed.

A few minutes later, she confronted a
surprised Steve at his front door.

"Hi," he said cheerfully. "Did you forget something?" He stepped back and let
her into the front hall.

"No — I mean yes," she blurted out. She
tugged at the zipper on her windbreaker.
Suddenly it seemed swelteringly hot inside,
and she wondered if she was coming down
with something. Steve was staring at her,

his blue eyes puzzled, as she tried to force the words past the lump in her throat.

"Yes?" he said encouragingly.

"I . . . Steve. . . ." She swallowed hard. "Look, I feel really silly asking you this. . . ." She crossed her fingers behind her back, and closed her eyes. "But would you go to the Halloween Dance with me?"

For an awful minute, there was dead silence. She was afraid to move, afraid to even breathe, but she finally opened one eye in time to see a big grin spread over Steve's face. "Hey, sure, I'll be glad to go."

"You will?" Nora said with surprise.

"Sure, I will," he said, throwing an arm around her shoulder. 'Why didn't you ask me before? We're pals, aren't we?"

She shook her head, not trusting her voice. "Just silly, I guess," she finally managed to say. "It's two weeks from Saturday — "

"I know when the dance is," he interrupted her. "And I'm really glad you invited me, Nora." He paused. "It'll be a blast."

The same words she had told Jennifer! She couldn't believe her luck — it was all so easy.

"Okay, see you then. I mean . . . I'll see you before but I'll also see you then," she said, stepping onto the front porch. She forced herself to sound casual, as if it was the most natural thing in the world to ask a boy out on a date.

She waited until she heard the front door close behind her and then she giggled with relief. She'd done it!

"You look like you're plotting something," Nora told Jennifer a couple of days later. They were eating lunch in the school cafeteria with Tracy Douglas and Amy Williams, and Jennifer had one eye on her macaroni and cheese and one eye on the serving line. She jumped guiltily when Nora spoke to her, and dropped her fork.

"Who me?" she gulped. "Of course not." Jen gave a funny little laugh. Just then she saw Steve Crowley at the end of the line and she felt a prickly sensation at the back of her neck. Could she do it? Could she really get up the nerve to ask him to the Halloween Dance? She felt dizzy with embarrassment just *thinking* about it, but what was the alternative? If she didn't ask Steve, she'd have to go with one of the creeps out of the yearbook!

"Then what are you staring at?" Nora craned her neck to see what Jennifer found so intriguing.

"Nothing," Jen said, too quickly. "I'm just trying to decide if I want some dessert." She forced herself to smile even though her insides were churning. How had Nora ever gone through this? she wondered. When Nora had gleefully confessed that she had a date for the dance, Jennifer had gone into a state of panic. If Nora could do it, *she* could do it, she reasoned. Not only *could* do it, but *must*! And time was running out. . . .

"They've got rice pudding today," Tracy said, licking her spoon appreciatively. "It's really good. I think it's the kind out of a can."

"Rice pudding — that's exactly what I feel like," Jennifer said, jumping up. "It's been ages since I've had rice pudding."

Nora stared at her in astonishment. "But Jen, you hate rice pudding! You always say it's the one thing that Jeff makes that you can't stand."

"I do?" she said confusedly.

"You sure do," Nora said with a laugh. "You say all those raisins in it remind you of dead flies." She nudged Tracy. "Look at that expression — she's up to something."

"Honestly, Nora," Jennifer said, irritated. "You're imagining things." She scooped up her tray and squirmed out of her chair. "Be right back," she said.

"Wow," Amy Williams said, "I've never

seen anyone get so excited over dessert before."

"There's got to be more to it than that," Tracy Douglas said slyly. "In fact, if I didn't know better, I'd say that Jennifer is after one of the guys." She tapped her Coke glass with her long magenta fingernails. "Look, she's in a huddle with the Big Three right now."

"The Big Three?" Nora swung around in her chair to get a better look.

"The three cutest guys in school," Tracy explained. "Mitch Pauley, Tommy Ryder, and Steve Crowley. They're all standing in line together — and look at Jennifer. She's hanging over the rail, trying to get their attention." Tracy opened a tortoiseshell compact and smeared on a thick coat of Tender Peach lip gloss. "You were right, Nora," she said, smacking her lips together and checking the effect. "She's definitely up to something."

"What looks good for dessert?" Jennifer was saying in her brightest voice. Three pairs of male eyes swung to her, and she almost lost her nerve.

"Dessert?" Mitch Pauley asked.

"Yeah, dessert," she repeated. "Like the gooey stuff on the plates behind you."

She put one hand on her hip, the way she'd seen Tracy Douglas do, and tried a giggle. "I'll just have to close my eyes and pick something, I guess." She ducked her head under the rail that divided the serving line from the tables and came up just inches away from Steve Crowley.

"Eenie, meenie, miney, mo. . . ." She gave a gay little laugh, and swept up a dish of rice pudding.

"Jennifer, are you all right?" Steve said. His melting blue eyes were concerned.

"Why, of course I'm all right," she said loudly. Then she bit her lip in consternation. "Except . . . I need to borrow a quarter from you. I left my purse in my locker."

"No problem," Steve said, digging into his pocket. He handed her a coin, and started to push his tray along when she stopped him.

"I'll write you an IOU," she offered.

"Hey, don't be silly," he said with a laugh. "I think I can trust you for a quarter."

"No, I insist," she answered a little wildly. Before he could stop her she whipped a pen out of his shirt pocket and grabbed a napkin. She wrote rapidly and then tucked the napkin in his pocket. "Guard this with your life, and call me tonight," she whispered, and quickly moved toward the cashier.

Her heart was beating so fast, she was sure it was going to leap out of her chest, but somehow she managed to pay for the rice pudding, and make her way back to the table. When she sat down, she felt a wave of doubt sweep over her. The note probably wasn't the best way to approach him, she decided. Maybe she should have waited until she got him alone . . . but what if someone else beat her to it?

She tried to imagine what Steve would think when he read the hastily scribbled words, but that only made her more nervous, so she gave up and turned her attention to the rice pudding.

She took a timid bite and remembered why she hated it. It tasted just like wallpaper paste. With flies in it.

After dinner that night, Jennifer raced to her room, locked the door, and waited for the phone to ring. When the call finally came, she forced herself to wait for the fourth ring. No sense in being too eager.

"Hello?" she said, in what she hoped was just the right tone — friendly, yet casual.

"Jennifer, I'm glad I got you," Steve

said hurriedly. "I can only talk for a second because I'm late for practice — "

"Oh, that's okay," she purred. "Did you . . . um . . . read my note?"

"That's what I'm calling about." Steve's voice suddenly sounded hesitant — maybe even a little embarrassed? — and Jennifer's fingers tightened on the receiver. "I really appreciate your asking me to the Halloween Dance," he began, "but — "

"But you're already going with someone else," she blurted out.

"That's it exactly," he said. He sounded grateful at being let off the hook. "Someone else asked me a couple of days ago. Otherwise, you know I'd go with you. . . ."

"Oh, sure," said, trying to keep the disappointment out her voice.

"But maybe the four of us can get together at the dance."

"The four of us?"

"Nora and me, and you, and . . . whoever your date is."

Jennifer was puzzled. "Nora?" she asked. "I don't think I understand — "

"Nora's the one who asked me."

Jennifer was so stunned she couldn't speak for a moment. Nora had asked Steve Crowley — and never said a word to her! She felt her throat tighten with anger.

"Sure, that'll be fun," Jennifer said in

a brittle voice. "We'll all have to get together."

When she hung up, she sat curled up in the bean bag chair. Nora was her best friend, and yet Nora had gone behind her back and invited Steve to the dance.

"Oh Nora," she said softly, "how could you do this to me?"

"You look terrible, Jen," Nora said cheerfully the next morning. "Were you cramming for the French test? You look like you've been up all night."

Jennifer had rehearsed exactly what she would say to Nora, but now that she was facing her in the bustling school corridor, the words flew out of her head. She had planned on being calm and decisive, and was horrified when she felt hot tears spring to her eyes.

"I just made an absolute idiot of myself because of you!" she blurted out. "I can't believe you did this to me, Nora Ryan."

"Jen, what's wrong?" Nora reached out to touch her arm, but Jennifer jumped back as if she had been burned. "What's happened?"

Jen took a deep breath. "I just found out that you asked Steve Crowley to the Halloween Dance."

Nora's face cleared a little. "Oh, darn

it, he shouldn't have told you — it was supposed to be a surprise. But I still don't understand what the problem is."

"The problem," Jennifer said tightly, "is that I asked him, too!"

Nora's mouth dropped open. "Oh, no," she said softly. "I didn't know you were going to do that."

"Oh, yes," Jennifer said sarcastically. "I guess you thought you were pretty smart, beating me to it."

"Pretty smart? What in the world—" The rest of Nora's sentence was drowned out by the homeroom bell. "Look, you're not making sense," Nora began when the bell finally stopped.

"Just forget it!" Jennifer quickly brushed her hand over her eyes and stalked down the corridor. "You asked him, and he's going with you, and that's it. There's nothing left to talk about."

"Jen!" Nora cried, hurrying to catch up with her. "What are you so mad about? We agreed we'd surprise each other." She was baffled. Why was Jen so furious?

"I'm mad because . . . because you *tricked* me," Jennifer shot over her shoulder. "You went through all those pages in the yearbook with me, and deep down you *knew* you already had a guy in mind — Steve."

"No, it wasn't like that, honestly. I just made up my mind at the last minute to ask Steve and—" Nora broke off suddenly and her expression changed. "What am I apologizing to *you* for? *You* asked him, too!" She gave a harsh laugh. "Some friend *you* are!" As soon as the words were out of her mouth, she wanted to take them back, but it was too late.

Jennifer's eyes turned frosty. "That's funny, I was going to say *exactly* the same thing to you," she said coldly. And without another word, she turned and disappeared into the crowd.

The next four days were the worst that Nora had ever spent. The nightmarish scene with Jennifer kept playing over and over in her head, like some continuous videotape. Everything was etched in sharp detail—the cold looks, the angry words, and worst of all, the tape always ended the same way. Their friendship was shattered.

"There's got to be a way out of this mess," she said to her mother one afternoon after school. The final meeting of the theme committee had just broken up an hour earlier and Jennifer had deliberately stayed away.

"I never thought things would turn out

this way," her mother said sympatheti-cally. "You and Jennifer were such good friends." She pulled a bar stool up to the gleaming kitchen counter, and cradled her coffee mug in her long, slender fingers. "I don't know why Jennifer took this thing with Steve so . . . personally. All three of you have known each other for years."

"That's the awful part," Nora confessed. "Now that I've had a chance to think about it, I can see why she felt so hurt and be-trayed. She thinks I went behind her back and asked him."

"But didn't she do the same thing?" Mrs. Ryan pushed a plate of chocolate chip cookies toward Nora, who shook her head. "Oh c'mon, have one, you'll feel better," Mrs. Ryan urged.

Nora took a cookie and bit into it thoughtfully. "She didn't *really* do the same thing," she said. "You see, when she asked Steve, she knew I already *had* a date. I didn't say who it was, because that was part of the game."

"Some game," her mother said lightly. "By the way, who did Denise ask to the dance?"

"Timothy Marks," Nora answered. "And he happens to be the best-looking boy in school."

"How about your other friends?"

"Amy thinks she's got a date, but she's not sure. Lucy thinks the whole thing is crazy, and Tracy has asked *three* boys. She's going to wait till the last minute to decide which one to go with."

"It sounds like Denise has really stirred things up."

"She's ruined everything!" Nora cried. "I wouldn't be in this fix if it weren't for her," she added resentfully.

"Are you still planning on going with Steve?"

Nora shrugged. "Not unless something works out for Jennifer. I couldn't enjoy myself if I knew she was sitting home alone. We've been friends too long."

"You know what I think?" her mother said, wiping off the counter. "I think it's time to call a truce."

"She won't talk to me, Mom. I've tried to see her at school, and she just walks away like I'm invisible."

"Then go to her house," her mother said practically. She reached over and ruffled Nora's short brown hair affectionately. "She can't walk away from you there."

Chapter 14

Half an hour later, Nora found herself standing on Jennifer's doorstep, trying to get up the nerve to ring the bell. What should she say — should she apologize? What she did wasn't really so terrible, was it? Certainly not worth breaking up a friendship over.

She was rehearsing her opening lines: "Jennifer, I really need to talk to you," when the door suddenly swung open, and Jennifer's younger brother, Eric, came barreling out. Jennifer was right behind him, bundled up in a cherry-red jacket, her long black hair swept back in barrettes. When she saw Nora, she gasped in surprise.

"Jennifer, this is crazy — I've got to see you," Nora blurted out. Now that she had gotten the first words out, she had no idea what to say next.

Jennifer looked at her silently for a moment, and then said, "I'm going with Eric to the park." Then she said in a little voice, "You can come with us, if you want to."

"Okay," Nora said, trying to keep her voice even. She jammed her hands in her pockets, and she and Jennifer fell in step together as Eric went skipping on ahead. "It's turned cold," she said, as they crossed Woodburn Street and headed for Greatneck Park.

"You should have worn gloves," Jennifer said. Then she gave a hint of a smile. "It's not like you to forget things."

"It's been a tough week," Nora said seriously. They were quiet until they reached the park, and then they sat side-by-side on adjoining swings.

"Nora, I—" Jennifer began, just as Nora spoke up.

"Jennifer, I—"

Then they both fell silent.

"You go first," Jennifer said after a moment. She spun around very slowly, letting the swing unwind itself.

Nora licked her lips. "I . . . uh, just wanted to say that I'm sorry about what happened." She glanced up at Jennifer who was suddenly preoccupied in picking a loose thread off her black wool gloves. "I *never* would have asked Steve to the dance if I had known you were interested in him."

"I'm not *interested* in him," Jennifer began.

"Interested in *asking* him, I mean," Nora said quickly. "Look, Jen, the only reason I asked Steve is — " she grinned sheepishly " — I couldn't think of anyone else to ask." She paused, and thought she saw a hint of a smile lurking on Jennifer's lips. "Those guys in the yearbook were pretty hopeless, you've got to admit."

"Even Charlie Parker?" Jennifer teased.

"You mean Charlie the Tuna — he was gross!"

Jennifer started to giggle and quickly suppressed it. She sneaked a look at Nora. Her *best* friend, she said to herself. "Nora, I'm sorry about what happened, too." Her voice was shaky, and she felt hot tears start to well up behind her eyes. "I never wanted to argue with you — "

"Me, either!" Nora said.

"I don't know how this whole crazy thing came about . . ." Jennifer went on.

I do. It was Denise, Nora longed to say.

"But one thing I do know — we can't break up our friendship over it."

"Then let's declare a truce," Nora offered. She reached out her hand to Jennifer, who clasped it tightly. "No more crazy arguments," she said, wiping away a tear that threatened to spill down her cheek.

"No more secrets," Jennifer added, squeezing her hand. She jumped off the swing and embraced Nora in a quick hug.

Nora buried her face in Jennifer's red jacket and felt a wave of relief wash over her. She had her best friend back! Suddenly she knew what she had to do. "And no more dates for the dance," she said tightly. "That's what started this whole thing."

"But you already have a date —" Jennifer said, bewildered.

"Not anymore," Nora said, jumping to her feet. "I'm going to call Steve the minute I get home and tell him I've changed my mind."

"You mean we're not going to the dance after all?"

"Oh, we're going all right," Nora told her, grinning from ear to ear. "But we're going the way we always do — as singles. And you know something? We're going to have a blast!"

"Hold still, will you?" Nora muttered through a mouthful of pins the following Saturday night. She was kneeling on the hard oak floor in Jennifer's room, doing her best to hem Jennifer's lion costume.

"I am holding still!" Jennifer complained. "But honestly, Nora, we're going to be late for the dance. Can't you take bigger stitches or something? You're not doing major surgery." She shifted her weight restlessly from one foot to the other, and squirmed around until she could see herself in the dresser mirror. She liked the way her costume had turned out. The fuzzy fake fur remnant she'd bought at Walton's had been just the right size for a jumpsuit, and there was even a piece left over to make the tail. She'd added a bright orange dime store wig that stood up in spikes all over her head and used Tawny Tan makeup on her face.

"It would be easier to do major surgery than this," Nora said. "At least the patients stay still for you."

"You're not making the legs too wide, are you?" Jennifer asked nervously. She made a sudden movement and Nora stuck her with a pin. "Ouch!"

"No, I'm not making the legs too wide," Nora said calmly.

"You're so lucky you managed to borrow a dance costume from Sally," Jennifer said. "You make a beautiful ballerina."

"Thanks," Nora muttered, struggling to her feet. "I think the toe shoes were a mistake, though. I don't know how she even walks in these things — they've got a block of wood inside!" She hobbled painfully to the mirror in the pink satin shoes, and Jennifer stood next to her.

Jennifer threw an arm around her shoulder and smiled at her in the mirror. "I think we look fantastic," she said, beaming.

"We look pretty good," Nora agreed. "Except . . . weren't you supposed to have a tail?"

"Omigosh!" Jennifer said, as she scrambled through a shopping bag and pulled out a long, furry tube. "Here it is — I stuffed it with Kleenex."

"Very realistic," Nora said. "But I wish you had told me before. Now I'll have to thread the needle again."

"No, that's okay," Jennifer said hurriedly. "Here, just pin it on." She handed Nora a small gold safety pin. "I don't want to be late."

"Are you sure it will stay on?" Nora said doubtfully. "You'll have to be careful and not move around too much."

"Of course it will stay on," Jennifer said gaily. "Nothing could go wrong tonight!"

"Have you seen Denise?" Tracy asked excitedly in the Cedar Groves girls' room half an hour later. "She looks gorgeous!"

"No, we just got here," Nora said. "We haven't gone into the gym yet." She brushed her short dark curls and fastened a rhinestone tiara on top of her head. She heard the pulsing sounds of Duran Duran drift in from the gym, and butterflies started to dance in her stomach.

"Well, you won't even recognize it," Tracy went on happily. "The decorations are fabulous and there must be a ton of food. Denise was right — this is going to be the best dance Cedar Groves ever had." Tracy had gone for the Western look and was sporting a fringed leather vest, tight blue jeans, and a toy holster with two six-guns. She saw Nora staring at her and said, "I'm supposed to be Annie Oakley."

"You look very nice," Jennifer said. "Did you finally decide on a date?"

"I've got four of them," Tracy giggled. "I guess I got carried away!"

Lucy came in just then, wearing a green hospital scrub suit and a surgeon's mask. A stethoscope dangled from around her neck and she playfully put it next to Tracy's heart. "Mmm, just as I suspected," she said seriously. "You're lovesick."

"Did you bring a date?" Nora asked.

"It's just Jimmy Bartley . . . and, well, to be honest, he's my cousin," Lucy told her. "We came as a team, and if you want to get a laugh —" she started to giggle uncontrollably " — just go out and take a look at him in a hospital gown."

"Oh, no!" Tracy squealed. "I can't believe it." She headed for the door just as Denise swept in.

"What's this — the conference room?" Denise said kiddingly. She was wearing an extravagant orange-and-white cat costume.

"Your costume is beautiful," Jennifer said admiringly. "It's so realistic — you look exactly like a giant cat."

"One of my father's friends does the costumes for a Broadway play," Denise said casually. "They had an extra one in stock, so they sent it to me." She touched up her lipstick, and tucked a stray lock of blonde hair back inside the furry cap. "There's lots of single boys in the gym," she said encouragingly. "Why don't you get out there and dance?"

"We were just going to," Nora said, trying to sound confident. She looked at Jennifer and the same thought crossed their minds: They had stalled long enough. "Are you ready?" she asked Jennifer.

"Ready," Jennifer answered. She felt really nervous, and wondered if Nora felt the same way. It was one thing to see boys in school, but another to face a whole gymnasium full of them!

"Then let's go," Nora said, moving toward the door. Jennifer stepped into the hall first, and then three things happened at the same time. There was a rumbling noise, a piercing scream from Jennifer, and a terrible ripping sound.

Nora looked up in time to see Jason Anthony careening down the hall on his skateboard, an evil grin plastered on his freckled face. "Nora!" Jennifer wailed. "He ran over my tail!"

"Oh, no," Nora said, bending down to look at the damage. Jennifer was missing not only her tail, but a square of material from the seat of her costume.

Jen ducked back into the girl's room and pulled Nora with her. "What am I going to do?" she cried. "I can't go out there like this!" She picked up the limp tail and looked at it sadly. "I can't even pin it back on — it's in pieces."

"What's going on?" Lucy said, puzzled. "It sounds like the roller derby out there."

"Jason Anthony and his skateboard," Jennifer said furiously. "He's ruined everything for me. I'll have to go home and change."

Denise took in the situation at a glance and said calmly, "No, you don't. We'll just have to switch."

"Switch?"

Denise reached behind her and unsnapped the lush, furry tail from her own costume. "That's lucky. The safety pin is still stuck in the material," she said, inspecting the seat of Jen's pants. "No one will ever know the difference." She quickly pinned the tail in place and stepped back. "There," she said, looking pleased. "It's not a bad match at all. It's even the right color. I better get back to my date now," she said, heading for the door. "He'll think I've met somebody else."

"Wait a minute," Jennifer said stunned. "You can't give me your tail. You've . . . you've ruined your costume."

"No I haven't," Denise said with her hand on the door. "I'll just pretend I'm a Manx cat — they don't even have tails." She smiled and darted out the door before Jennifer could say another word.

A few minutes later, Jennifer and Nora were standing by the buffet table in the crowded gym, trying to look as if they were having the time of their lives.

"What do you think?" Nora asked, spearing a meatball on a plastic fork.

"It's beautiful," Jennifer said brightly. "No one would ever believe that this is where we have PE." She looked at the dance floor, trying to pick out familiar faces. The combination of the flickering strobe lights and the costumes made it difficult to tell who was who. She spotted Tracy Douglas slow-dancing with a boy dressed like a skeleton and smiled. Colored light bulbs revolved slowly over Tracy's head, turning her long blonde hair from orange to green to red. Her partner didn't seem to mind dancing with a rainbow-haired girl, though, because he suddenly pulled her close, and Jennifer looked away, embarrassed.

"You don't seem very hungry," Nora said, pointing to her plate. "You're letting your pizza get cold."

"No, it's fine," Jennifer said, forcing herself to take a bite. It tasted like cardboard smeared with ketchup, but she gulped it down and reached for a Coke. She didn't want to admit that her insides were churning. What was she doing here anyway? She knew she couldn't spend the whole evening hanging over the buffet table with Nora, but what else could she do? She didn't want to end up on the dance floor like Tracy . . . did she?

"You're wasting some great music," Lucy Armanson said. She danced by with her partner — a tall boy in a white hospital gown — and gave a little wave.

"She looks like she's having fun," Jennifer said.

"She sure does," Nora agreed. Lucy makes it look so easy, but of course, Jimmy is her cousin, Nora thought to herself. For the past few minutes, her mind had been running on the same track as Jennifer's. We can't stand here forever, a little voice inside her warned.

Nora was about to say something when Mitch Pauley tapped her on the arm. "Do you want to dance?" he muttered, not looking at her.

For a moment she was too surprised to answer. Mitch still had his eyes glued on the dance floor, and she noticed he was wearing his football uniform.

"Go ahead," Jennifer whispered, and nudged her forward.

"Uh, sure, I guess so," Nora gulped.

When Mitch took Nora's hand and tugged her toward the center of the room, Jennifer felt suddenly panicky. Now what am I going to do! she thought. I'll look like an absolute idiot standing here alone.

At that very moment, Amy Williams appeared at Jennifer's side. She was dressed as a vampire, and had some very realistic-looking fangs protruding from her mouth. "You don't have a date, either?" she asked hopefully.

"Do you mean it *shows*?" Jennifer asked.

"Well, you know what they say. It's

better to go to a dance without a guy — that way, you can choose whoever you want."

"Mmm," Jennifer said, unconvinced.

"The food sure looks good," Amy said longingly, her eyes wandering over the buffet table.

"Why don't you have something?" Jennifer said absently. She was watching Nora and Mitch Pauley out of the corner of her eye as they danced to a Rolling Stones song.

"Are you kidding — with these fangs?" Amy gestured to her Coke. "I'll have to stick to a liquid diet tonight." She tugged thoughtfully at one of the fangs. "I suppose I shouldn't have used that Super Glue — my mom says if I can't get them off tomorrow, she's going to kill me." She suddenly pointed to the doorway and squealed in delight. "Look, there's Mia Stevens and Andy Warwick — they came as *preppies!* I don't believe it — I never thought I'd see Andy wearing *argyle!*" She gulped the rest of her Coke. "I'll see you later, okay? I've got to check this out!"

"Have fun," Jennifer said cheerily. The moment Amy was gone, she dumped her pizza plate in the trash bin and took a deep breath. She had to move — now!

She decided to make a circle of the room, pretending she was looking for someone.

If she walked slowly, and kept to the edges of the gym, it would take at least fifteen minutes, she decided. She glanced at her watch. It was only nine-thirty. That meant she'd have to circle the room ... *eight times* to fill up the whole evening! She groaned inwardly and started on the first lap. At least I'm not wearing toe shoes like Nora! she thought gratefully.

Then Steve appeared next to her. "Want to dance?" he asked, somewhat nervously.

Jen nodded her head and they walked to the center of the gym. The music was slow, and when Steve put his arm around Jennifer's waist, she suddenly felt embarrassed. Usually, they could talk without any problems, but tonight they seemed to have nothing to say to each other.

What's happened? Jen thought. Just because this is a bring-a-date dance does that mean that even friends get funny with each other? But she knew that was it. Once they got back to school everything would be fine. But right now she wasn't sure how to act. The school had had a lot of dances and *boys* had been there, but this dance was different.

Steve cleared his throat and said, "Good music. Don't you think?"

Jen looked at him and said, "I hate it. I hate this dance."

Steve laughed and everything was all right again. "Let's get something to eat. Denise has provided a banquet."

At that moment, Nora was wondering if it was possible to fall asleep standing up. She was dancing a slow dance with Mitch Pauley, and he was whispering football scores in her ear. There was something almost hypnotic about the combination of the soft music and the monotonous voice that made her feel as if she were drifting on a cloud.

"You should have seen the way Harold carried the ball in the fourth quarter," Mitch murmured. "It was the third down and eighteen on our own twenty," he said eagerly. "They came in a blitz! Harold took off 'round the weak side and ran forty-five yards...."

"Forty-five yards," Nora repeated dully. She gave herself a little shake to clear her head. She had to stay awake!

"And that was just the beginning," Mitch said, encouraged. "The next play he caught a touchdown pass ... that made it fourteen-thirteen with ten seconds to go."

"Wow," Nora said softly. The good thing about Mitch, she thought, was that he didn't need much feedback. Just an interested grunt now and then.

A vision in orange and white fluttered

by — Denise Hendrix and her date, Timothy Marks. They made a perfect couple, Denise's blonde beauty contrasting with Timothy's dark good looks. They looked special, grown-up, Nora decided. They looked like they belonged together. Denise was laughing up at Timothy, looking *so* sophisticated. So at ease. Nora reluctantly turned her attention back to Mitch Pauley, who was still talking about the amazing Harold. What in the world was she doing dancing with him? She sneaked a look at her watch. Another hour and a half to go! This was going to be the longest night of her life.

"It was really fun, wasn't it?" Nora said brightly to Jennifer later that evening. They were dressed in pajamas, sitting up in bed in Jennifer's room, passing a bowl of popcorn back and forth.

"It sure was," Jennifer agreed. "I'm glad you could sleep over tonight. I figured we'd have tons of stuff to talk about."

"Oh, absolutely. Tons," Nora said, reaching for a handful of popcorn.

For a moment, there was dead silence while Nora munched popcorn, and Jennifer started to remove the Frosted Beige nail polish she had worn to the dance.

Jennifer cleared her throat. "Thanks for

hemming my costume tonight — you did a great job."

"That's okay, I was glad to," Nora told her. "It was just lucky that Denise came through the way she did." She shook her head. "I never thought she'd mess up her own costume for you." She paused. "I saw you dancing a couple of times. I tried to catch your eye, but the gym was so crowded. . . ."

"I know," Jennifer said, inspecting her fingernails. "I saw you on the dance floor, too. You seemed to be having a good time with Mitch."

"He's a very good dancer," Nora said seriously. "And he really knows a lot about sports. You wouldn't believe the things he told me about defensive strategies. And tackling! He could practically write a book on it."

"Hmm," Jennifer said, scrunching a pillow behind her head. "It sounds fascinating."

"Oh, it was," Nora said quickly. She drew her knees up to her chest and wrapped her arms around them. Jennifer's room was a little chilly and she was glad that she had packed her red Dr. Denton's with the feet.

"Do you . . . uh, think you'll see him again?"

"See him again?" Nora looked puzzled.

"I mean . . . do you think you'll start dating him or anything like that?"

"Date Mitch Pauley!" Nora hooted. She fell back on the pillow laughing. "You've got to be kidding! I was so bored I nearly died! The guy doesn't have two brain cells to rub together, and — " She stopped suddenly, her cheeks flaming.

Jennifer was staring at her in shocked surprise. "So you didn't have a good time, either?"

Nora twisted a brown curl around her finger, the way she always did when she was thinking. "I had a rotten time," she said finally. "In fact, it was one of the worst nights of my life. Everyone was so stiff and . . . weird."

"I'm glad to hear it," Jennifer said, with a faint smile on her face. "I thought I was the only one who was a little weird." She tucked the covers around her. She was wearing a yellow Garfield nightshirt with short sleeves, and white crew socks.

"What do you mean, weird?"

"Well, I just felt really out of it tonight. Everybody else seemed to be having a terrific time at the dance," Jennifer explained. "And I felt like I wanted to drop through the floor." She paused. "I didn't know what to do or who to talk to — "

"You danced with Steve. I saw you," Nora said.

"*Steve.* Steve is from kindergarten days," Jen answered.

"But you were dancing with Terry Garrison," Nora interrupted. "I saw you with him, too."

"Only because he spilled a Coke on my costume," Jennifer said. "He tripped over my tail reaching for a meatball."

"No!" Nora howled.

"Yes, I'm afraid so," Jennifer laughed. "I think he felt so guilty, he asked me to dance with him."

"And I thought you two were starting a great romance," Nora teased her.

"And I thought you and Mitch Pauley were madly in love," Jennifer retorted.

"Please, not while I'm eating!" Nora pleaded. "The only reason he asked me to dance is that he was supposed to go to the dance with Shirley Hayden, and she got the flu."

"You're sure that's all there was to it?"

"I'm sure," Nora said grimly. "He probably figured I was the only one there who hadn't heard all his dumb football stories." She emptied the popcorn bowl in her hand and said thoughtfully, "Denise seemed to be enjoying herself. I guess she's used to going to dances and dating and every-thing."

"I guess so." Jennifer picked a loose thread off her white chenille bedspread. "Nora, what do you think about her — really?"

"Really, truly?" Nora said kiddingly. "She's okay, I suppose. I really liked the way she helped you out with your costume tonight — "

"But?" Jennifer questioned.

Nora sighed. "But she's so different than we are, Jen. She seems so much older — she's been everywhere and done everything. I know you want to be friends with her, but I just don't think we have that much in common with her. You saw her tonight. She knows what to say to boys. I wish I did. She's different from us, Jen."

Jennifer was quiet for a moment. "I feel the same way, Nora. I didn't realize until I saw her tonight, dancing with Timothy. I'm just not ready to start dating and doing all the things she does. I'm not ready to be like her, I guess."

"Well, we don't have to be," Nora said. "We can just be ourselves, can't we? That's the great part of being in junior high. Everything's ahead of us — we don't have to rush it."

"Do you think we'll want to ask boys to the next Halloween Dance?"

"I don't know," Nora said seriously. "That's a whole year away — anything could happen." She looked at the clock and scrambled to her feet. "There's something going on right now that we shouldn't miss, though."

"There is?" Jennifer sat straight up in bed, puzzled.

Nora flipped through *TV Guide* and turned on Jennifer's portable TV.

"Oh, no, not another vampire movie," Jennifer moaned. "Nora, don't you ever get enough of those things?"

"Never," Nora said, rapidly flicking the dial. "This one's a classic — "

"Don't tell me, let me guess," Jennifer muttered. "It's the one about the lady vampire who meets a werewolf."

"Exactly!" Nora said, pleased. 'Our minds are on the same track." She looked at the empty popcorn bowl. "There's only one thing missing," she said forlornly. "Just one thing that would make me completely happy. . . ."

"I know, I know," Jennifer griped, sliding out of bed. "A gigantic bowl of hot popcorn, with extra butter and salt." She threw on a robe and headed for the kitchen, just as the opening credits of the movie filled the screen. "Don't bother getting up," she said wryly.

"Okay, great," Nora said eagerly, and jumped back in bed, her eyes glued to the screen. "I'll fill you in on anything you miss." She looked at Jennifer who was jamming her feet into terry slippers. "And Jen, thanks a lot."

Jennifer turned with one hand on the doorknob. "That's okay, Nora," she said. "After all, what are best friends for? *But*, next time *you* make the popcorn."

The ringing of the phone in the hall startled both the girls. They both ran to it. "Who do you suppose it is?" Nora asked.

Jen picked the receiver up. "'Lo." Suddenly, her face contorted and she stuck her tongue out, and held the receiver away from her ear so Nora could listen, too.

"It's me, gorgeous, irresistible Jason Anthony. I just didn't want either of you two girls to lose sleep tonight because I didn't get to dance with you. Next Halloween dance, I promise I'll devote myself to you."

"Thanks a lot, Jason," Jen said and hung up.

As the girls walked back to the bedroom, Nora said thoughtfully, "You know, Jen, maybe we should just skip next year's dance."

JUNIOR HIGH

Coming soon . . .
Junior High #2
CLASS CRUSH

Will Cedar Groves Junior High survive a class crush?

"I am madly, impossibly, one hundred percent, head-over-heels in love," announced Jennifer Mann, flashing her hazel eyes.

Nora Ryan looked across the cafeteria table at her best friend and laughed. "I take it you sort of like the guy." Then she got all dreamy. "He *is* gorgeous, isn't he?"

Susan Hillard, Tracy Douglas, and Mia Stevens banged down their lunch trays, making Jen and Nora jump.

"Don't be too sure he'll even look at *you*," said Susan sharply, sitting down. "*I've* read both his favorite books, so I *know* we have something to talk about."

186

Tracy was puzzled. "Who ever said anything about *talking* to him?" she asked. "I just want to *look* at him."

Mia put down her fork and sighed, running her fingers through her orange hair. "Do you think *he'll* look at *me* if I dye this mop fuchsia?"

"You could try," Nora said seriously. Jen was about to agree when the bell rang.

Who are the girls in love with? How will they get him to notice them? And what will Steve Crowley, Mitch Pauley, and the other eighth-grade boys do about the incredible class crush?